CITY FARM

Zoe and Swift

CITY FARM

Books in the
City Farm series…

Zoe and Swift

Jessie Williams

Special thanks to
Linda Chapman

First published in 2013 by Curious Fox,
an imprint of Capstone Global Library Limited,
7 Pilgrim Street, London, EC4V 6LB
Registered company number: 6695582

www.curious-fox.com

Text © Hothouse Fiction Ltd 2013

Series created by Hothouse Fiction
www.hothousefiction.com

The author's moral rights are hereby asserted.

Illustrations by Dewi@kja-artists

ISBN 978 1 78202 021 9

1 3 5 7 9 10 8 6 4 2

A CIP catalogue for this book is available from the British Library.

Typeset in Baskerville by Hothouse Fiction Ltd

Printed and bound CPI Group (UK) Ltd, Croydon, CR0 4YY

MIX
Paper from
responsible sources
FSC
www.fsc.org
FSC® C020471

To Deb and Andy Jones – for the advice, encouragement, support and for being such good friends. And to all the horses out there like Swift who help people more than they know.

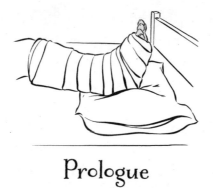

Prologue

Zoe stared at the white ceiling. She had pulled the curtains round her bed, shutting out the busy ward with the nurses bustling about, the parents talking, the little kids playing. With the curtains closed, she felt like she was in her own little world. She wished she could stay there. She didn't feel like ever going outside again.

Catching sight of the plaster cast that covered her right leg from her knee to her toes, she shut her eyes. Her mind filled with pictures of the last race she'd run. She remembered the feeling of speed, passing the other runners, crossing the finishing line. Afterwards her coach had come up to her and told her that if she kept running like that she'd be in the Olympics one day. It had been one of the happiest days of Zoe's life.

She'd been daydreaming about the Olympics in the car on the way home – and then someone had driven into Mum's car.

The doctors had explained that her leg had been so badly broken that she would have to wear a cast for several months. She would then have to have physiotherapy and would probably walk with a limp for the rest of her life. It would be a long time before she raced again, if ever.

Lying there, Zoe felt empty. Like everything inside her had been ripped away, leaving an empty, hollow space. Tears started to creep down her cheeks. She scrubbed them angrily away.

'Hi, sweetheart.'

The curtains pushed aside and Mum looked in. She looked like an older version of Zoe, tall and skinny with dark skin and long braided hair. She was smiling, but Zoe could see the strain in the lines around her eyes.

'Hi, Mum,' Zoe managed, having to force the words past the lump in her throat.

'Well, today's the big day. It's time to come home.' Mum smiled brightly.

Zoe bit her lip as she thought about going back to her house. She was looking forward to going home, but she felt funny about it too. It would be like nothing had changed, when everything had.

Her mum must have seen the misery on her face. 'Oh, Zoe,' she said softly, crossing to the top of the bed and fiddling with Zoe's braids. 'I know it's really hard for you but you'll feel better when you get back home. I promise you will. We've made the study downstairs into your bedroom now so you won't have to go up the stairs and you'll soon feel like your usual, cheerful self. Things will start getting back to normal.'

'Normal?' Zoe said bleakly.

'Yes, normal.'

Zoe turned her head away. Her mum was trying to be nice, she knew that, but she had no idea. Absolutely no idea at all. Normal? No. One thing was for sure. Her life was never going to be normal again...

Chapter One

Jack ran into the farmyard at City Farm, dodging the clucking chickens that were pecking happily at the weeds and scratching at the ground. He raced past the stone barn, which doubled up as an office and café. The sheep and goats bleated hopefully at him from their pens but he didn't stop – not even to take a quick look at Curly the sheep and her lamb, Lizzie. Jack usually loved going round all the animals when he first arrived, saying hello to each and every one of them, but that day he wanted to get to the stable block as quickly as possible. A new horse was coming to the farm and there would be lots to do to get ready for it.

As he splashed straight through a puddle in his old green wellies, happiness bubbled up inside him. It was the weekend. No school for two days. No reading or writing to get muddled up with. Just helping with the animals and seeing his friends.

The farm was right in the middle of the city. Surrounded by houses and concrete tower blocks, hemmed in by the railway lines and roads, it was a little oasis. The farm was open to the public and lots of people came to visit the animals and sit in the café eating the delicious home-made cakes that the volunteers cooked. But City Farm wasn't just for day visitors. It was also the home of the Harvest Hope project – a scheme set up for kids like him who were having problems either at home or school, or kids like his friend Asha, who was recovering from being ill.

The main stable block was at the far end of the farmyard. It had four stables in it and was made of stone with a slate roof. It was old and a section of the roof over the two stalls at the end had fallen away and was patched up with a green tarpaulin. The doors had ancient black bolts and the old white paint on them was chipped and scratched. The top halves of the doors were open. Stanley, a black and white pony, was looking out of one of the stables, dropping stalks of hay as he munched. He whinnied when he saw Jack.

Jack ran over and rubbed Stanley's shaggy neck. 'Hey, boy. How are you today?' The pony nuzzled

Jack's sandy hair with his lips. Jack grinned and ducked away. 'Oi! My hair's not hay!'

Hearing his voice, Dusty, the farm donkey, looked out of the stable next to Stanley and brayed noisily. Jack went over to say hello to him too, just as a girl looked out of the tumbledown stable at the end. She had a broom in one hand and was wearing a blue hat. 'Jack!' she said, her face lighting up.

'Hi, Asha!'

Asha was very thin but her brown eyes were bright and sparkling. She was recovering from having leukaemia, and she was getting better every day.

'So you finally decided to get here, did you?' she teased. 'I set my alarm clock for seven o'clock so I've been here ages! I've been cleaning out the stable we're going to use for the new horse.' The words bubbled out of her. Sometimes it was hard to get a word in edgeways because she spoke so much! 'Come and see!' she urged.

Jack followed her and looked into the stable. 'You've done loads!'

Asha beamed with pride. There were four stalls in the old stable block – the ones that Dusty and Stanley lived in, one that was used as a storeroom and one that was empty because the roof leaked. Only yesterday the stall Asha was cleaning out had been piled high with junk – old rugs and bits of tack, gardening tools and ancient buckets. Now it was empty apart from a dusty feed manger in one corner and a bucket and broom.

'Everything that was in here has gone into the stable next door,' Asha explained. 'That's going to be the main storeroom now. Rory has put up some tarpaulin to try and mend the leak so that everything doesn't get wet. And' – she added excitedly – 'I found some bunting in here when I was clearing up.' She pulled a string of red and blue bunting from the manger. 'I thought we could put it up to welcome the new horse. First, though, we've got to get rid of all the dust and cobwebs. After that, Rory says we need to disinfect the floor.'

'Did someone mention my name?' boomed a voice.

Rory came striding towards the stable, a bucket of water in one of his giant hands and a metal tin of disinfectant in the other. Rory Trent was the City Farm manager. He was in his sixties with bushy white hair and a face that was tanned and weathered from his years spent outdoors. 'Morning, Jack. Good to see you, lad. You looking forward to meeting our new resident, then?'

'Oh, yes!' said Jack. Apart from Stanley, he hadn't seen any horses since he had come to live in the city. 'So what's the horse like?' he asked Rory, as he started sweeping up the cobwebs and dust from the stable floor.

'He's an ex-racehorse called Swift,' Rory replied. 'He's too old to race now and so his owners have decided they don't want him any more.'

'Just because he can't race?' Asha said, sneezing as Jack swept up a cloud of dust. 'That's mean.'

Rory sighed. 'Ay, I'm with you on that, Asha. They retrained him so that he could give rides, but he didn't make enough money doing that, so they decided he had to leave. To some people animals are just a business. Anyway, I said we'd make room for him here. It'll be good for Stanley to have some more horse company. Horses are happier when they have friends.'

'Like people!' Asha grinned at Jack.

Jack smiled back at her. 'I can't wait to see him,' he said.

'It may take him a bit of time to settle in,' said Rory. Swift has lived all his life on a busy racing yard. It's going to be a very different life for him here. We'd better give him lots of TLC.'

'TLC?' said Asha, frowning. 'What's that?'

'Tender Loving Care,' translated Jack with a grin. His grandad had often used the same expression.

'Well, we can definitely give him heaps of that!' Asha declared.

'Who's going to give heaps of what to who?' said a bright voice. Kerry Barker came into the stable. Kerry was the Harvest Hope co-ordinator. She looked as different from Rory as it was possible to be, with her bright red padded jacket that matched her lipstick, and tiger-print wellies. That day her long black braids were trimmed with red and gold beads that jangled as she walked.

'We were just saying Swift's going to get lots of love from us,' Asha told her. 'We'll make sure he's happy.'

'And not just Swift,' said Kerry. 'We've got another new arrival coming later this morning too – a human one.'

Jack felt a flicker of worry. He was always a bit worried about someone horrible joining the Harvest Hope programme. 'Who?'

'A girl called Zoe Clarke. She was in a bad car accident,' explained Kerry. 'She's hurt her leg and is on crutches. She's coming here because her parents are worried about her. She's always been very popular and confident, but since she got out of hospital she's been quiet and depressed.'

'Is she getting bullied at school?' Jack asked sympathetically.

'No,' Kerry replied. 'I think it's more to do with the fact that before her accident she was a serious runner, but now it doesn't look like she will ever be able to run competitively again. Even when her leg has healed she'll probably be left with a limp. She's finding it hard to adjust.'

'Oh no!' said Asha. 'Well, being here will be good for her. No one can be sad for long with all the animals to look after!'

'Just remember, though, that some people love it here straightaway like you did, but others take a bit longer,' Rory said gently. 'Don't expect miracles with Zoe on her first day.'

Kerry nodded. 'She's got a lot to get her head round at the moment.'

'So? We'll cheer her up!' said Asha, shooting a grin at Jack. 'I just *know* we will!'

Chapter Two

Zoe's mum parked next to an ancient barn. It had a ridged roof and small diamond-paned windows. With the moss coating its tiles, it looked almost as if it was growing out of the ground. Hanging baskets filled with bright red geraniums swung from hooks along the wall and smoke came from the chimney.

Zoe opened the car door and looked at the farmyard. So this was City Farm. It was the middle of the morning and there were quite a few people walking around in the sunshine – mothers pushing buggies, toddlers holding hands with their grandparents as they strolled in and out of the barns and peered into the pens. Zoe gazed around – it was so pretty it was hard to believe that they were still in the middle of a city!

'So, here we are.' Mrs Clarke came round and helped Zoe out, handing her the crutches that she had to use now when she wanted to get around.

The first thing Zoe noticed as she stood up was the smell of animals. She could hear them too – goats bleating, a cockerel crowing, ducks quacking from a nearby pond

What am I doing here? she thought, as she gingerly put her weight on her crutches. *I can't do anything to help on a farm. Not with my leg like this!* She glanced down at the plaster cast on her right leg. Her jeans had been cut off at the knee so they would fit over it and her toes were sticking out of the bottom of the cast. Her mum had made her put a thick sock on, and had taped a carrier bag over the sock so that it wouldn't get wet or muddy if she had to put her foot down in the farmyard. It didn't even feel like her leg any more.

Mrs Clarke looked around anxiously. 'Now, I wonder what we have to do? Can you see anyone else?'

Zoe felt butterflies flutter in her stomach when she thought about meeting the other kids on the Harvest Hope project. Before the accident she had spent all her free time with people from her athletics club. All she knew about was running – what would she talk to the other Harvest Hope kids about?

'Are you all right, love?' her mum fussed. 'How's your leg feeling?'

Really bad, Zoe thought. She opened her mouth to say, '*Take me home, Mum.*' But before she could speak, the door of the barn opened and a lady in a bright red jacket came out.

'Mrs Clarke?' she asked, hurrying over to greet them. 'And you must be Zoe. I'm Kerry Barker, Harvest Hope co-ordinator. It's lovely to meet you at last.'

Kerry had such a warm smile that Zoe couldn't help but like her.

'Come into the barn and then we'll have a look around,' said Kerry. 'After that, you can get started with some jobs, Zoe. There's always lots to do here – animals to be fed, stalls to be cleaned, eggs to be collected.'

Zoe felt a flicker of excitement. *Those things actually sound like fun!*

'I'm sorry, Kerry, but Zoe won't be able to do any of that,' her mum interrupted. 'She finds it very hard to just walk at the moment.'

'Oh, don't worry, we'll find something for her to do,' Kerry said cheerfully. 'Now, do come into the office.'

Zoe moved slowly on her crutches. She was only just getting used to using her upper-body muscles to support her weight and her arms and shoulders ached. The ground was slightly uneven which made it harder for her. Her right crutch hit a pebble and wobbled.

'Are you all right?' Her mum put a hand out to steady her. 'You know, maybe this isn't such a great idea, Kerry,' she said suddenly. 'Zoe's only been out of hospital for a little while. When I heard about the Harvest Hope project, I thought the fresh air might do her good, but maybe that was a silly idea. She can't really help much on a farm. She's very fragile still.'

Kerry's voice was reassuring. 'Please don't worry, Mrs Clarke. Zoe will be just fine here with us. In fact, I'm absolutely sure she'll have a great time. Now, you've already filled in the paperwork at home and sent it back to me, so why don't you leave us to it? Kids often settle in better here without their parents worrying about them.'

'Well ...' Mrs Clarke hesitated anxiously. 'What... what do you think, Zoe?'

Zoe hesitated. *Maybe I should just go home with Mum... ?* she thought.

But then Kerry smiled at her. 'You'll be fine – it'll be a challenge,' she said with a wink.

Zoe took a breath. 'I'll … I'll be fine, Mum,' she managed to say.

'I promise I'll ring you if there are any problems,' Kerry said gently to Zoe's mum. 'And you can call me at any time if you want an update on how Zoe is doing today.'

Mrs Clarke nodded reluctantly. 'Perhaps it is for the best if I go, then.' She kissed Zoe's forehead. 'Bye, poppet. Be good. I'll be back to collect you at four o'clock.'

'Bye,' Zoe whispered, trying her hardest to be brave. But watching her mum walk to the car, she suddenly felt very alone.

Kerry squeezed her arm. Zoe saw understanding in her brown eyes. 'I know it feels hard, but you'll soon settle in. Now, come in and we'll get you sorted out with a welly for your left foot.'

As Zoe entered the barn, she caught her breath. She'd thought it would be big and empty, but it was the cosiest space imaginable. The walls were covered by lots of children's drawings and there was a black wood-burning stove with two comfy sofas and a desk at the far end. The air was filled with the sweet scent of wood smoke. 'Oh, wow!' she said, looking around. 'This is lovely.'

Kerry smiled. 'This is the office where we have meetings and where we all come to warm up if it gets cold outside. Do you like animals, Zoe?'

'Oh, yes,' Zoe said.

'Good,' said Kerry. 'You're going to be meeting quite a lot of them here, from Curly the sheep to Cynthia the pig.'

'Cynthia!' Zoe smiled. 'That's a funny name for a pig!'

'Don't let Jack hear you saying that,' said Kerry. 'He's also on the Harvest Hope project. He's animal-mad and he's completely dotty about Cynthia. He even gave her a football to keep her amused.'

A footballing pig! City Farm was full of surprises. Zoe couldn't help feeling curious about what Kerry was going to say next.

'So, first things first,' said Kerry. 'What size wellies do you wear?'

'Size four, please,' Zoe told her.

Kerry went over to a low shelf by the door and started rummaging round. She came back over with a green welly. 'Here you go. This should fit you.'

Zoe lowered herself awkwardly onto a chair and held her good foot out, waiting for Kerry to help her put it on like her mum did at home. But Kerry just put the boot down next to her. Zoe didn't like to ask her to do it, so she leaned forward in her chair awkwardly, reaching out so that she could position the boot and slip her foot into it.

'Well done,' Kerry said quietly, as Zoe took hold of her crutches again and stood up. 'Now, time to get you outside and find some things for you to do.'

'But what can I do out there?' The words burst out of Zoe before she could stop them. 'I'm useless, look at me!'

'You are *not* useless, Zoe Clarke!' Kerry said firmly. 'Come on. I didn't think you'd be the sort of person who gives up when things are tough. You had to be pretty strong to run all those races – I bet you didn't give up then.'

Zoe shook her head.

'OK, you might be not be able to push a wheelbarrow or brush the yard very well at the moment,' Kerry continued, 'but you can groom the animals, help feed them, and put their beds down. So what if it takes you a bit longer to get around the place, I'm sure the animals won't mind! What do you say?'

Zoe looked at Kerry's kind eyes and gave a little nod. 'I'll try,' she agreed.

'Great.' Kerry smiled. 'That's all we ask. Now, let

me show you around and then I'll introduce you to Jack and Asha. They're getting ready for someone else new who is starting today.' Kerry's eyes twinkled and she gave a secret smile. 'He's called Swift.'

'Who's Swift?' Zoe asked curiously.

Kerry smiled mysteriously. 'Ah, you'll have to wait and see!'

Chapter Three

Zoe followed Kerry out into the farmyard. Kerry pointed to an uneven gravel path that led away from the barn. 'Down that path is the garden and vegetable plot, and Cynthia's sty. We'll stick to the main farmyard for now though, as it'll be easier for you on your crutches. Let's start with the small animal barn.'

She headed to a shed that had a picture of rabbits and guinea pigs painted on the door. Zoe hobbled along beside her, feeling mixed up inside. It was nice that Kerry seemed to believe she would be able to do things – if she was honest, she had to admit she was getting a bit fed up of everyone at home running around after her and not letting her do anything – but she couldn't help worrying that she might let Kerry down. Mum was always telling her to remember that she wasn't as strong as she used to be.

Kerry opened the shed door. It was warm inside and Zoe breathed in the smell of animals. 'We keep the guinea pigs and rabbits here,' Kerry explained. 'There's always lots of cleaning out and feeding to do – and cuddling, of course! The rabbits and guinea pigs are all very tame and like lots of attention.'

There were four wooden pens in the middle of the barn and a bench and cupboards round the outside where the food and bedding was stored. Two of the pens had rabbits in, one had guinea pigs and one was empty. The animals looked very happy. In one pen a mother rabbit and two smaller ones were hopping around. One of the babies was the same orangey-brown colour as the mum and one was cream-coloured. In the pen next door a big milky-coloured rabbit was snoozing in a pile of hay, while the guinea pigs in their pen were squeaking and chasing each other through some piping. They had golden fur and one had brown patches.

'Oh, the little rabbits are really cute!' Zoe said, forgetting her unhappiness for a moment as she looked at the cuddly youngsters, with their soft coats and twitching noses.

Kerry smiled. 'The mother is Peaches. The babies

are Crumble and Custard. The rabbit in the next-door pen is the dad, he's called Cream.'

'Peaches, Custard, Crumble and Cream!' said Zoe, smiling despite herself.

Kerry took some chopped-up pieces of carrot out of a Tupperware container in one of the cupboards and added some to the pens. Her eyes twinkled. 'How do you know carrots are good for your eyes?' she asked Zoe.

'I don't know,' said Zoe in surprise.

'Because you don't see any rabbits or guinea pigs wearing glasses!' Kerry chuckled and Zoe giggled. 'That's one of Asha's favourite jokes,' Kerry went on. 'She's on the Harvest Hope programme too and she loves the rabbits and guinea pigs – particularly the guinea pigs. You know, it's strange but everyone always ends up having a favourite animal here. I wonder what yours will be?'

Zoe wondered too. She loved animals, but she'd never had a pet – she had spent too much time running to be able to look after one properly.

Kerry interrupted her thoughts. 'Let's have a look at some of the other animals now.'

They went outside and looked at two goats in a pen. They had white coats and curly beards and looked quite cheeky. They put their heads though the rails of the pen and 'meh-eh-ed' eagerly. The slightly bigger one stuck his head through the bars and pulled at Kerry's coat with his teeth.

'Stop it, Billy!' scolded Kerry. 'That's Billy, he's very naughty. Bramble is quieter. The girl goats, Nellie and Nancy, are out in the fields for the day with Dusty the donkey. He's a bit grumpy – I'm sure you'll hear him "ee-yore-ing" as you go around the farm.'

There were so many animals to meet that Zoe's head whirled with all their names. Finally they reached a tumbledown stable block at the far end of the farmyard. It looked quite scruffy with its partially patched roof and old stable doors, but a cute-looking shaggy pony had his head over one of the doors and someone had hung cheerful red and blue bunting from one side to the other.

'Looks like Asha and Jack have been working hard,' said Kerry, nodding at the bunting. She frowned. 'I wonder where they are?'

Just then the end stable door flew open and a thin girl wearing a hat came running out, followed by a boy with sandy hair and a sopping wet sponge in his hand.

Zoe felt a pang of jealousy as she watched them

chase each other around. Once she would have been able to run and dodge as easily as that. Now she was stuck on her crutches.

The girl dodged as the boy threw the sponge. 'You missed!' she said triumphantly, as it hit the floor with a splash.

'Wait till next time,' he told her.

'Asha! Jack!' Kerry called.

They suddenly realized they had an audience. Asha ran over. Jack followed with a slightly more cautious look on his freckled face.

'Hi, you must be Zoe!' Asha said enthusiastically. 'Kerry told us you were coming today. Welcome to City Farm.'

Her smile was so wide that Zoe couldn't help but smile back. 'Hi,' she said.

'Do you like the bunting?' Asha chattered on. 'We put it up for you – well, you and Swift. He's a horse who's arriving today too. Rory's just gone to get him. We thought you and Swift might both like it. I can't wait to see him. Oh, I'm so glad you've come. You're going to love it here, Zoe! Everyone does!'

Zoe blinked, a little overwhelmed by Asha's enthusiasm. 'Right … um … thanks.'

'Don't mind Asha,' said Jack, seeming to understand.

'She never stops talking.'

'I do so!' Asha cried.

Jack winked at Zoe. 'OK, maybe when you're eating – or asleep!' he teased.

'Take no notice of him,' Asha told Zoe.

Zoe felt some of her worries melting away. She'd been dreading meeting the other kids and trying to make friends, but Jack and Asha seemed normal and nice. She wondered why they were at City Farm. There didn't seem to be anything wrong with them.

'Asha, can you make sure that the bunting is nice and tight, so that it doesn't flap in the wind and scare Swift?' Kerry said. 'Horses don't like noises like that.'

'OK.' Asha nodded.

'Well, I'll leave you to it,' Kerry smiled. 'I've got work to do, phone calls to make. You'll be fine,' she said to Zoe. 'Asha and Jack will look after you and tell you what to do and Swift – the new horse – should be here soon. I think you're going to have a lot in common!'

How could I have something in common with a horse? Zoe thought. But before she could ask any questions, Kerry headed off towards the barn. 'See you later,' she called back over her shoulder.

'So, what would you like to do?' Asha asked Zoe.

'Shall we show you around?'

Zoe felt awkward. Her arms were hurting from using the crutches and there was a familiar ache in her leg. It wasn't a good ache, like when she'd run a race and her muscles were tired but happy. This was a deep-down hurt. 'Kerry's shown me lots already and I'm a bit tired now.'

'Well, we've got to put straw down in the stable for the new horse,' said Jack. 'Do you want to help with that?'

Zoe bit her lip. 'Um … well, I would,' she said, not wanting them to think she was unhelpful, 'but I don't think I'll be able to with my leg.' She gave him and Asha an apologetic look. 'Sorry, I'm rubbish, I know.' *I didn't used to be like this*, she wanted to add. *I used to be able to run really fast and win races.* But she'd never say that. It would be too boastful.

'Well, you can sit down and maybe help out anyway?' Asha suggested. 'If we carry the straw, could you scatter it in the stable?'

'Yeah, and we can tell you all about the farm,' said Jack.

'Great, thanks!' Zoe said.

They all went into the stable. It was clean and empty and smelled slightly of disinfectant. Zoe settled down against one wall, her leg out in front of her. There were two big squares of compressed straw in a wheelbarrow, Jack and Asha emptied them out and pulled them over to where Zoe was sat. Then they carefully pulled off the ties round the straw and they all shook it up so that there was a big fluffy pile. Zoe grinned as the straw got looser and bits of dust shone and shimmered in the air.

'Did you see all the animals, even Cynthia?' Jack asked.

'I didn't see her, but Kerry told me about her. She's a Tamworth pig, isn't she?' Zoe said.

Asha nodded. 'Which other animals did you like?'

'I liked all of them,' said Zoe. Asha beamed. 'Particularly the sheep and her little lamb,' Zoe went on. 'And the guinea pigs and rabbits were really cute.'

'I love the guinea pigs!' said Asha.

'You love *all* the animals,' Jack laughed, as he spread the straw around on the floor. 'We still need more,' he continued, putting the prongs of the fork through the straw and hearing the ping of metal as the fork hit the concrete below. 'You shouldn't be able to hear any noise from the fork when you do that. I'll go and fetch another bale.'

He set off with the wheelbarrow, and Asha sat

down next to Zoe. 'So what's the horse like, the one who's coming here?' Zoe asked Asha.

'I don't know much about him, only that he's an ex-racehorse called Swift,' answered Asha, sitting on an upturned bucket. 'He can't race any more so he's coming to live here.'

An ex-racehorse. Zoe felt the pieces of the puzzle click into place. So that was why Kerry had said that she and the horse had something in common. They both used to race but neither of them could any more. Zoe felt for the horse. 'Poor thing, I bet he really misses racing.'

'Kerry said *you* used to run in races before your accident,' Asha said.

'Yeah.' Zoe let herself remember for a moment. 'It was amazing. I loved it. I could just forget myself and run and run. And then when I crossed the finishing line first…' She broke off and swallowed. 'I guess I'm never going to feel like that again.'

'Isn't your leg going to get better?' Asha asked.

Zoe shrugged. 'The cast will come off in a month or so, but I'll probably always limp. I won't be able to run in races, not like I did before.' She felt a lump form in her throat and had to swallow hard. She didn't want to cry in front of Asha.

'That's awful,' said Asha sympathetically. 'At least you can still walk.'

Zoe could tell Asha didn't understand. 'You don't know how much I used to run,' she blurted. 'I mean, when you do something every day, it's your whole life … I dreamed of being in the Olympics. I used to run in a club after school and race every weekend. All my friends were running friends. Now I never see them.' Zoe felt tears welling up in her eyes.

'You could go and cheer them on?' Asha suggested. 'And if they won't do something else with you, then they're not proper friends anyway.'

'I guess…' Zoe said, her throat tight.

Just then Jack came in. 'Sitting down, Asha? That must be a first!' He shook his head and looked at Zoe. 'Asha's supposed to take it easy, but she never does.'

'I don't like sitting around!' said Asha.

Zoe looked at Asha curiously. 'Why are you supposed to rest?'

Asha gave a matter-of-fact shrug. 'I had leukaemia,' she said. 'The treatment made my hair fall out. It's why I wear a hat or scarf all the time.' She reached up to touch her hat self-consciously. 'I'm OK now, but I've got to build my strength back up. Everyone always fusses about me but I'm fine.' She jumped off the bucket as if to prove it. 'I've got loads of energy!'

'You still need to remember you've been ill,' Jack told her.

'Why?' Asha gave him a quick look, her face serious for once. 'Why do I need to remember? I could be in hospital, but I'm not – I'm lucky. I don't want to be poor, sick Asha. I don't want to sit down and be fussed over. I just want to do things and have fun.'

Jack held up his hands. 'All right, all right. Why don't you shake up the straw, then.' He emptied the bale of straw out of the wheelbarrow.

As Asha started work, Zoe felt bad about making a fuss over her leg and her friends. She'd had no idea Asha had been so ill. She didn't know much about leukaemia, but she knew it was serious. Feeling a bit ashamed, she pulled herself to her feet and started scattering the straw around. *Asha's been really ill, but she's getting on with things. I should be more like that*, she thought.

Kerry's voice called to them. 'Zoe! Asha! Jack! Rory's back with the horse trailer.'

'Swift's here!' Asha said, her brown eyes lighting up. 'Quick! Let's go and meet him. Oh, I wonder what he'll be like!'

Chapter Four

Asha ran out of the stable and then skidded to a halt. 'Oh, sorry!' she said, as she looked back at Zoe hobbling on her crutches. 'You can't go very fast, can you?'

'It's OK,' Zoe said quickly, not wanting to hold her back. 'Go on ahead.'

But Asha and Jack both shook their heads. 'We'll walk with you,' said Jack.

Zoe felt a happy glow as she made her way slowly across the farmyard with the two of them beside her.

'Do you know anything about horses?' Asha asked her.

'Not really, although I used to be crazy about them when I was little, before I started running,' Zoe admitted.

'I've never even sat on a horse,' Asha told her.

'I used to live on my grandad's farm, so I've ridden horses,' Jack told her. 'I'm not that keen though.' He smiled. 'I prefer the pigs. How about you? Have you ever ridden at all?'

'Just a few times,' Zoe said. 'I've been pony trekking on holidays and had some pony rides. I'd love to do more but there's never time for me to have proper lessons, not with all my running practice and—' She realized what she'd just said. 'Well, there never *used* to be time,' she corrected herself. 'I guess I'll be able to do more things now.'

A battered Land Rover had stopped in the car park, pulling an old grey horse trailer that looked like it had seen better days. A tall man with a cloud of white hair was undoing the bolts on the back ramp and talking to Kerry. As he lowered the ramp, a loud whinny echoed from inside the box.

Zoe felt a shiver run down her spine. She couldn't wait to meet Swift.

'That's Rory,' Jack said, pointing at the man.

Rory went into the trailer and a few seconds later a horse came backing out with a clatter of hooves, Rory holding its lead rein. It was wearing big, protective boots on all four legs.

'Oh,' Zoe breathed. The horse was beautiful. He had a white stripe on his face. His chestnut coat was dusty and a bit muddy but he held his head proudly as he looked around the farmyard. He stood very still for a moment and then swung in a circle.

'Isn't he gorgeous?' cried Asha, hurrying to greet him.

'Wait, Asha!' Jack grabbed her arm. He was just in time. He pulled her out of the way as the horse shied back, darting away from her.

'Steady now, lad, steady!' Rory soothed.

Asha stopped, horrified. 'I didn't mean to scare him!'

'It's all right.' Kerry put her arm round Asha's shoulders as Rory calmed Swift by walking him in circles and patting him. 'You didn't know, but you need move slowly around horses. They can often be nervous, especially when they arrive somewhere new.'

'Ponies like Stanley are different,' Jack explained. 'They don't often get scared, but thoroughbreds like Swift can be really jumpy.'

Swift scraped at the ground with one front hoof. Zoe thought he looked confused and anxious now. The excitement had gone from his eyes and he just looked bewildered. It was almost as though he had arrived somewhere he wasn't expecting…

Of course, she realized. That would be exactly what had happened. He was used to arriving at a racetrack. The tumbledown farm must look very strange to him. He'd be wondering what was going on. She longed to go over and stroke him, but she didn't want to scare him with her crutches.

Jack and Asha approached him cautiously. 'You are getting yourself into a state, aren't you, boy?' Jack said softly, looking at the damp patches of sweat breaking out on the horse's neck.

'I reckon he was expecting to arrive at a racetrack,' Rory said.

I guessed that! Zoe wanted to say, but she bit it back. She didn't want to butt in or look like she was trying to be clever.

'He doesn't understand why he's here,' said Kerry.

'This is your new home, Swift,' Asha said to the horse as if he could understand. 'You're going to be very happy here.' The horse pushed her in the chest with his nose and then snorted. Asha giggled and wiped her jumper with her hands. 'Yuck!'

Swift pawed the ground anxiously again.

'You know, maybe he should go to his stable!' Zoe blurted out before she could stop herself. 'It might help him settle down?'

Rory threw a smile in her direction. 'I was just about to say the same thing, lass. So, you must be Zoe?'

Zoe nodded.

'I'm Rory Trent. Do you know much about horses, then?'

'No, nothing.' Zoe felt herself blushing.

'Well, you've certainly got the right instincts,' said Rory approvingly. He patted Swift. 'Come on, lad. Let's get these boots off and then I'll take you to your stable.' He leaned down and efficiently removed Swift's travelling boots, then led the horse off. The others followed. Zoe hobbled as fast as she could – she wanted to see what Swift thought of his stable.

Stanley whinnied a welcome when he saw the newcomer. Rory let the two of them touch noses to say hello and then he put Swift into his new stable and unclipped his lead rope. The chestnut horse walked round, sniffing the straw, ears pricked. After a few seconds, he swung round and thrust his head over the door. Asha tried stroking him but he pulled back. Jack produced a carrot and offered it to him but the horse wouldn't take it.

Zoe didn't go to the door with the others. She wanted to see Swift, but she didn't want to overcrowd him. She imagined how she would feel if she was him with lots of people trying to make friends all at once. There was so much for him to see and take in. Her heart went out to him.

'I think it's going to take a while for him to adjust,' said Rory.

'Maybe he would find it easier if he was just left with one person for a while,' Kerry said thoughtfully. 'I know we all want to help him, but I think it would be better for him if he just gets to know one person first. Zoe, why don't *you* look after him? Rory will stay nearby.'

Rory nodded.

Zoe gave Jack and Asha an anxious look. She was sure they'd want to stay with Swift too and she didn't want to upset them. 'I can always do something else,' she offered. 'I'd love to stay with him but I really don't mind. Jack or Asha can stay with him if they'd rather. After all, I can't do much with my leg.'

'You can talk to him, help him settle,' said Rory. 'And anyway I've got a job for Jack and Asha. I want to turn the spare run in the small animal barn into a play area for our guinea pigs Bubble and Squeak. You two will be happy getting on with that, won't you?'

'Oh yes!' Asha said eagerly. 'Bubble and Squeak

would love a play run!'

Jack nodded too. 'I've been doing woodwork at school. I could make them something. We could design the whole thing! And really' – he looked at the horse – 'it *is* best for Swift to just be with one person at the moment. I'd love to spend time here but we've got to do what's right for *him*.'

'Good lad!' Rory beamed. 'That's the attitude. So we're sorted. You two go to the small animal barn and start designing the play area, then we'll get to work making it.'

'And I'd better get on with some paperwork,' said Kerry. 'See you later, Zoe. I hope you can help Swift settle in.'

Zoe watched as Kerry, Jack and Asha set off up the yard and she was left with Rory and Swift. She couldn't believe Kerry had chosen her, but at the same time she felt a bit worried. She was on crutches. How could she possibly be the one to help settle the ex-racehorse in?

'Right, lass, the grooming kit's in here,' said Rory, going to the stable and opening the door to show Zoe a tack and storeroom. A couple of saddles were hanging on racks on the walls, bridles were hung up neatly on hooks and there were several feed bins, a pile of horse rugs in one corner and a couple of grooming kits in blue plastic boxes. Rory fetched one of them. 'Have you ever groomed a horse before?'

Zoe shook her head.

'Well then, you start with this brush. It's called a dandy brush,' Rory said, taking out a brush with stiff bristles. 'You use it to get off any mud, but go carefully – a sensitive horse like Swift might find the bristles a bit tough. You might find it easier to use this rubber currycomb.' He showed her a circular piece of rubber that had rubber bumps all over it. 'After you've got rid of the mud you use a body brush to brush his coat. You always brush in the direction his coat grows and every few strokes you have to clean the brush with this.' He picked up a metal grooming tool with little metal spikes and showed Zoe how to scrape with the spikes to get out the dust and grease from the bristles. 'That's the basics and a groom will really help Swift settle and feel much better – he's got quite sweaty in the trailer. Right.' He hung the grooming kit on the end of Zoe's crutch. 'I'll just tie Swift up in the box with a hay net and then leave you to it.'

'But…' Zoe protested. 'I … I—'

'You'll be fine,' Rory reassured her. 'Just use those instincts of yours, they seem pretty spot on to me.'

He loosely tied the horse's lead rope to a loop of twine on a ring in the stable, hung up a string net of hay and, with a wink to Zoe, strode away.

Zoe swallowed and turned back to the stable. 'Well,' she whispered, 'it's just you and me now, Swift. I guess I'd better get started.'

Chapter Five

Swift had moved back as far as he could so that he was close to the back of the stable. He looked at her but didn't come over. Zoe hobbled towards him, wanting to stroke him, but as soon as she got close he seemed to shrink back even further against the wall. Zoe stopped. She could read the message that was clear in his eyes: *go away.*

She thought back over the last few weeks. She'd been so miserable, as she'd tried to get her head around what had happened to her. She remembered the constant stream of visitors who had come to the hospital and then to her house and sat with her, hugging her, talking to her. Sometimes it had been nice, but at other times she'd just wanted to yell at them to leave her alone. Swift looked as if he was feeling the same thing now.

Use your instincts. Rory's words echoed through her mind.

Zoe made a decision and took a step back. If Swift wanted to be left alone then she wouldn't try and force him to get to know her. The bucket that Asha had been sitting on earlier was still in the stable, to one side of where the hay net was hanging. She lowered herself onto it with difficulty and laid her crutches on the floor behind her. 'If you don't want me to groom you, that's fine,' she said softly to the horse. 'I'll just sit here for a while instead. I bet I couldn't help the others much with the play stuff they're building anyway, so I might as well just stay here with you.'

The horse's ears flickered at the sound of her voice. Zoe watched him. He was so beautiful but his dark chestnut coat was dirty and his mane and tail were tangled. He didn't look like he'd been brushed in a while. She imagined how he would have been as a racehorse. She'd seen racehorses on TV. They always looked immaculate, their coats shining, their manes plaited, their tails silky soft. If Swift had been used to all that attention, what must it have been like for him when he had stopped racing and stopped having all the grooming and fuss?

'It must be so hard,' she said softly. 'I bet you don't understand at all, do you, boy? The racing's just stopped and you don't know why. At least I understand why *I* can't run. I know what it's like, wanting to run and not being able to. It's horrible, isn't it?'

Swift didn't understand her words, but he seemed to like the sound of her voice and the fact that she was sitting down and not crowding him. He snorted softly and then took a step nearer her. From her position sitting on the bucket he looked incredibly big and his hooves seemed as wide as dinner plates, but Zoe stayed where she was. She couldn't have moved easily, and anyway she just felt sure Swift wasn't going to hurt her.

He moved closer and reached down with his enormous head.

'Hello,' she whispered. She gently touched his cheek. There was a patch of mud encrusted there. Zoe rubbed it away and then quietly stroked down his nose and smoothed his short forelock. Swift lifted his muzzle to her face and blew in and out softly, sniffing her just as he had done with Stanley. Zoe realized it must be his way of saying hello.

She tentatively reached up to stroke his face. In that second, she felt a connection spark between them and the rest of the world seemed to fade away. She'd never felt anything like it, but for a few moments it was just her and Swift and they completely understood each other. Swift snorted gently and lowered his muzzle until it rested on her shoulder. She stroked the white stripe on his face. 'It's OK,' she whispered to the big horse. 'I'm here. I understand.'

Zoe didn't know how long she sat there, stroking him, but in the end he sighed and lifted his head. Then he turned and pulled a mouthful of hay from his net and chewed on it. Zoe watched him for a moment and then struggled to her feet and fetched the rubber currycomb. She didn't want to use her crutches in case she scared him or she dropped one and it fell against him, so she hopped up to him, watching him carefully. He didn't shrink away this time so she took hold of his neck to balance and, using it to support herself, she started to groom him gently. Mud and hair came away in clouds. She sneezed but carried on.

Swift's ears flickered. She had the feeling he liked the sensation of the currycomb massaging his skin, cleaning his coat. Once she had done his neck, Zoe hopped to his side and then his hindquarters. He seemed to understand that she needed to lean on him to support herself and he stood very still, letting her work. By the time she had brushed him all over, her arms were aching and her face and clothes were coated in dust but Swift was looking cleaner. She refused to let herself stop. Starting all over again with the body brush and metal currycomb, she swept the brush over his whole coat.

'There!' Zoe said at last. 'You look much better!'

It was true. Swift's coat was free of mud and had a shine to it from the body brushing, his tail was now untangled and sleek. Zoe wrapped her arms round his neck and hugged him.

'Well, well, what a difference!' a voice boomed.

Zoe and Swift both jumped as Rory looked over the stable door. Swift retreated to the back of the stable.

'No need to look startled,' he said. 'You're doing a grand job, lass. I thought this fella would take several days to settle down, but give him an hour or so with you and he's as happy as Stanley next door!'

'Well, not quite,' said Zoe, standing awkwardly on one leg and using the toe of her injured leg to balance.

Rory saw her difficulty and came in and handed her the crutches. 'Maybe not yet, but he'll get there.' He gave her a thoughtful look. 'I was right. You are obviously a natural with horses.'

Zoe felt really pleased. She'd got so used to only

thinking of herself as a runner that it was lovely to think she might actually be good at something new.

'Let's get his feed,' said Rory. 'Then we can leave him to eat his lunch. You must be hungry too.'

Zoe realized that for the first time since her accident she *did* feel hungry. It must have been everything she'd been doing since she'd arrived at the farm – because she'd actually been allowed to do something energetic.

She followed Rory into the spare stable that was full of farm equipment. She noticed that the roof was patched and leaking and there were a couple of buckets on the floor to catch any rain water. Rory showed her how to measure out a scoop of something he called chaff, adding a smaller scoop of a feed he said was a coarse mix – a horse feed that looked a bit like dark muesli and smelled sweet. He mixed a little water into the bucket to make it easier for Swift to eat it, then gave her the feed. Zoe hung it on one of her crutches and hobbled back into the stable where she emptied the bucket into the manger as Rory untied Swift. The big chestnut horse came over and she stroked him as he ate.

'Well done,' said Rory with a smile. 'Now – lunch time!'

*

The rest of the day flew by. That afternoon, Zoe watched Jack and Asha finish off the play run for the guinea pigs. They had decided to build three platforms connected by tubes and ramps so the guinea pigs could run from one to the other. Jack was making all the platforms while Asha collected extra things the guinea pigs might like – smooth willow twigs to chew, some thick cardboard tubes that they could hide in, and a ball made out of rope that they could push around. Then she dotted bits of carrot and apple about the run to encourage the guinea pigs to explore. Zoe couldn't do much to help because a lot of what they were doing involved kneeling down and crawling around on the floor, but she chatted to them and handed them things as they needed them.

When the run was finished, Rory and Kerry came over to watch as they put the guinea pigs inside. Bubble and Squeak squealed in excitement and looked around, then Bubble – who was quieter – hid in a tunnel and Squeak – who had brown patches of fur on her golden coat – went exploring, pattering up the ramps and emerging from the tunnels, stopping to eat the tasty treats on the way.

'It's perfect!' Kerry declared. 'You've all done a great job. I bet the children who come and visit will love seeing them playing there, and Bubble and Squeak will be so much happier having more to do. Animals are much better-off when they are occupied.'

'I'm going to build a seesaw too, I think,' said Jack eagerly. 'And fix an exercise wheel in there.'

'Well done, all of you,' said Rory. 'Now, can you clear up here and then go and check the chicken shed for any eggs?'

'Sure,' said Asha.

'I'll tidy up here if you want, while you get the eggs,' offered Zoe.

Asha had shown her the chicken shed after lunch. It was a hut on stilts with a low roof. Zoe knew there was no way she could get in there with crutches.

'Thanks, Zoe.' Rory smiled at her. 'After that, you might want to go and check on Swift. I saw him just now looking over his stable door. I think he was watching for you.'

Zoe's heart swelled happily at the thought.

'Well?' Mum said anxiously, as Zoe hobbled towards her on her crutches at four o'clock. 'Have you been OK, poppet?'

For a second Zoe was confused about the worry in her mum's voice. She'd had such a lovely day it was hard to remember how anxious Mum had been that morning. 'Oh, it's been brilliant!' she said.

Mum looked hugely relieved. 'That's wonderful! I suppose it was good being outside even if you couldn't do much.'

'But I've done *loads*,' Zoe said enthusiastically. 'I helped Asha and Jack make a play area for the guinea pigs, and then Jack showed me how Cynthia plays football. Cynthia's a pig. And Mum, there's this amazing horse, Swift! I've been looking after him – grooming him and helping him settle in – and Rory says I'm a natural with horses.'

'Gosh!' Mum blinked at all the information. 'You'll have to tell me more about it on the way home. I'm surprised you've been doing so much. Do you think being here has helped you?'

'Oh, yes!' Zoe said happily. She thought about Swift. He'd let the others stroke him this afternoon, but it was Zoe he seemed to turn to, even when everyone else was there. It was wonderful to feel special – and to feel she was good at something again.

She got into the car and then looked round to see Kerry, Jack and Asha at the barn door. She waved. 'See you all tomorrow!'

'Bye!' shouted Asha and Jack.

'One minute before you go, Zoe!' called Kerry. She went inside the barn and came out with a book, which she brought over to the car. 'Hi, Mrs Clarke,' she said. 'Zoe's been great today. She's settled in really well and helped us so much. She's been a real credit to you – and herself.'

'Well, that's lovely to hear,' said Mum.

'I thought you might like to borrow this,' said Kerry, handing Zoe the book. It was all about horses and ponies. 'It's one of my old books – I used to have my own horse. We'll see you tomorrow, Zoe.'

'Bye,' Zoe said. 'Thanks for the book!'

She hugged the book as her mum drove off. City Farm was wonderful. She couldn't wait to come back again in the morning!

Chapter Six

After she had dinner, all Zoe could think about was reading Kerry's book. She hopped into her new room and made herself comfortable on the bed, with her bad leg stretched out in front of her.

Her new bedroom was on the ground floor. It was small and the windows looked out towards the garage wall. She preferred her old room upstairs with its view out over the garden, but she knew Mum worried about her going up and down the stairs. She was just trying to keep her safe.

Her leg itched, and she couldn't scratch it through the thick plaster. She took her mind off it by reading about horses. Soon she was completely absorbed. She learned about the different breeds and how to groom and care for horses, as well as all the different competitions horses could do. She found out lots about showjumping competitions where riders had to jump fences, and dressage competitions where horses had to perform a test of steps, like a dance routine. It was all fascinating!

Zoe went to bed with her mind full of horses. As she lay under her duvet, she realized that for the first time since the accident she felt light inside and excited about something. She had been able to help Swift and understand him. She'd groomed and fed him too. She pictured Swift in his stable and wondered how he was finding his first night at City Farm.

I'll see you tomorrow, she whispered to him in her head, and in her imagination he pricked his ears as he heard her voice.

When Zoe woke up she didn't lie in bed feeling miserable, like she had been doing since she had come out of hospital. She got up straightaway and used her crutches to get to her chest of drawers to get her clothes out. She carried them back to her bed and lay down to pull her jeans on. She wriggled into her T-shirt and then propped her cast up and pulled a sock on over it, feeling a flush of triumph that she had got dressed all by herself. She'd done it!

Her mum looked very surprised when she hobbled through to the kitchen. 'You're dressed!'

'Yes. I want to go to the farm. Can we go straight after breakfast please, Mum?' Zoe said eagerly.

Zoe's dad smiled. 'Hey, it's good to see you so keen about something again.'

'It's Swift. I want to go and see him,' said Zoe. 'He's so lovely, Dad. I'm going to ask if I can groom him again today.'

Her dad smiled. 'You know, you sound just like your old self. I'm really glad you're getting on OK at the farm.'

'I love it there!' Zoe beamed.

Mum shot her a worried look. 'That's good, but you will be careful, won't you?' she said, handing Zoe some breakfast. 'You won't do too much? Take plenty of rests and explain you can't do things if your leg hurts.'

Zoe nodded, but she felt determination bubbling up inside her. She wasn't going to take any rests at all or to tell people that her leg was hurting, even if it did. One of the things she'd liked best about City Farm was that no one fussed about her. They just expected her to get on with things like everyone else. She realized it made her feel better than when people were being anxious around her. 'I'll be fine, Mum,' she said. And this time she really meant it.

After breakfast, Mum drove Zoe to the farm and Zoe managed to pull herself out of the car without any help. 'Bye!' She went eagerly into the barn on her crutches.

Kerry and Rory were sitting on one of the sofas, drinking mugs of tea and reading some paperwork. 'Well, you're the early bird today!' said Kerry. 'It's very rare anyone beats Asha down here.'

'How's Swift?' Zoe asked.

Rory's weathered face creased into deep wrinkles. 'Not as good as I'd been hoping, lass.'

'Why? What's the matter with him?'

'He didn't eat all of his feed last night and he barely touched his hay. By the look of his churned-up bed he's had a restless night too.'

'Can I see him?' Zoe asked.

'Of course. You go on ahead to the stables.'

Zoe hobbled out of the warm barn. It was very quiet in the farmyard – not a single visitor was there yet and the café was only just opening up. Daisy, the old lady who ran it, was just starting to cook the first batch of cookies and cakes.

Stanley the pony was already out in the nearby field. Zoe looked over Swift's door. The big chestnut horse was pacing around his stable. 'Swift?' she called softly.

Swift's head jerked round and he came to the door, his nostrils quivering in a low whinny.

'Hi, boy.' Zoe stroked him. 'What's the matter?'

He pushed his nose against her, almost knocking her off her crutches, and then turned and started walking round restlessly again. Zoe noticed that his hay net was still full.

He came to the door again and accepted a quick pat before moving off round the stable once more. He really didn't look happy. Zoe wished he could talk to her and tell her what was wrong.

She watched him until Rory came to the stables. 'He's still not eaten anything, then,' said Rory, checking Swift's manger. 'There's nothing physically wrong with him. I've checked him all over. He's been pacing round since I got out here this morning and put Stanley out. Maybe we should try turning him out in the field with Stanley. That might settle him.'

Zoe nodded. She had read in the horse book how important it was for horses to go out in a field or paddock each day for some exercise if they could.

Rory fetched Swift's head collar and lead rope and led Swift out. The chestnut horse pranced beside him excitedly but he didn't pull on the rope too much. 'It's all right, lad. You're just going out in the field,' soothed Rory, his large hand patting the horse's neck.

As they reached the field, Zoe saw Swift's expression change. She was sure he looked disappointed.

Rory unclipped his lead rope. 'Go on, then!'

Stanley was grazing quietly under a nearby tree, but Swift didn't canter over to greet him. He didn't even put his head down to eat the grass. He just stood by the gate and whinnied loudly.

Rory shook his head. 'Hopefully he'll settle down soon. I'd better get on now. There's a feed delivery coming this morning and I need to get the goats sorted out…'

As he headed off, Swift came over to Zoe. He stared at her as if he was willing her to understand something. Zoe stroked his neck. She was sure he wanted *something* – and she was equally sure that whatever it was, it wasn't out in the field.

'Hey, Zoe!' Asha hurried towards her. She was wearing a bright pink scarf over her head that day.

'I like your scarf,' Zoe said.

'Thanks.' Asha looked self-conscious. 'My hair used

to be down to my waist, but now it's really short. Still, at least I'm not in hospital any more.' She looked up at the blue sky with white fluffy clouds floating across it. 'Imagine if you were trapped inside a hospital on a day like this.'

Zoe smiled. Asha always seemed to see the positive in everything. *I want to be like that again*, she thought determinedly.

'So, how's Swift?' Asha asked.

'Not great,' Zoe admitted. 'He didn't eat his feed this morning and he's very restless.'

'We could get him come treats,' Asha suggested. 'That might cheer him up. Some animal food's just been delivered – I saw some new sacks of apples and carrots in the barn when I arrived.' She grinned. 'We could also get ourselves some cookies from the café at the same time!'

Zoe smiled and they headed back up the farmyard together. The café had all its lights on now and the tables had been set up. As they walked in, Zoe breathed in the delicious scent of freshly baked cookies and flapjacks. Her tummy gave a rumble.

'Hi, girls! Are you hungry?' Daisy asked from behind the counter. She looked just like a jolly grandma with her curly white hair and a big happy grin.

'I'm starving!' said Asha.

Daisy smiled. 'That's just what I want to hear. You've got to build your strength up. Now I could do with a couple of tasters for my latest batch of chocolate chip cookies. My kiddies used to love these when they were little. Can I tempt you both?' She offered them a tray of fresh cookies. They were still warm and the chocolate chips had turned into deep melted pools of chocolate in the crumbly biscuit.

'Thanks, Daisy!' both girls said.

'Any good?' Daisy asked.

'Mmm,' Zoe said, her mouth full. 'Delicious!'

Asha swallowed. 'Actually, I'm not sure they're quite right, Daisy,' she said a mischievous glint in her eyes. 'I might just need to try another one to be sure…'

Daisy smiled. 'Go on. Take two each.'

The girls said thank you and took their cookies with them through the door that led into the barn. 'The carrots and apples are over here,' said Asha. She hastily dropped her voice as she saw that Kerry was sitting at the desk, deep in conversation on the phone. She led the way to where there was a big sack of carrots and a crate of apples.

As they filled a carrier bag to take back to the stables, Zoe couldn't help overhearing Kerry on the phone.

'I understand your position, Mr Jarvis, but it would be very helpful to know when this inspection will take place.' Her usually cheerful voice sounded strained. She paused. 'Yes, I understand that, but surely you can see my point of view. All I am asking for is a rough idea of when you will be visiting…'

'Come on,' Asha whispered and they left the barn, shutting the door quietly behind them.

'Who was Kerry talking to?' Zoe asked curiously.

Asha frowned. 'Derrick Jarvis. He's the Head of Finances or something like that at the council. He's horrible! He wants to shut City Farm down.'

'Shut the farm!' Zoe stared. 'But why would he want to do that?'

'He'd like to sell off the land so people can build houses and offices here instead,' said Asha. 'The land's really valuable and the farm costs the council money to keep going.'

Zoe looked around in disbelief. The day visitors had just started to arrive. The hens were pecking at the ground and she could hear the bleats from the goats as they competed for the visitors' attention. It was a perfect scene – a little bit of countryside right in the middle of the city. How could anyone possibly want to destroy it? 'He won't be able to shut the farm down though, will he?' she said.

'I don't think so,' said Asha. 'I can't imagine Kerry or Rory ever letting the council close City Farm.'

They went back to the field. Swift ate the treats, but he didn't seem much happier. Zoe watched him pacing up and down and wished she could work out what was wrong.

'Ah, there you are!' Rory said, coming over to the girls. 'Now, there's lots to be doing. Jack's just started the mucking out. Do you think you can give him a hand?'

'Sure!' said Asha.

Zoe nodded eagerly too, keen to help. *Today I'm going to do just as much as everyone else*, she thought positively. But when she started she found it harder than she'd imagined. Mucking out meant picking up the horse's droppings and the dirty wet straw with a pitchfork, while leaving the cleaner straw in a big pile. Zoe tried her best, but it was almost impossible to try and balance on one crutch and use a fork one-handed. Time after time she picked up a forkful of dirty straw and then as she tried to hop over to the wheelbarrow, she spilled it all over the floor again.

Although Jack and Asha were very encouraging, Zoe felt herself getting more and more frustrated –

she wanted to be able to do what they could, but she was just making lots of mess. Still, she made herself keep trying. *You can do it*, she told herself determinedly as she hopped across the floor.

'You're doing really well,' Asha said.

'Thanks,' Zoe sighed, stopping. 'But I feel like I'm making such a mess. It's hard to muck out on crutches.'

'Why don't you try helping with something else?' suggested Jack. 'The hay nets need filling up. You could do that. The hay's in the store next door.'

Zoe went to the storeroom. There was a large bale of hay there and two empty hay nets made of nylon string on the floor. Resting her right crutch against the wall, she supported herself on her left crutch and picked up the hay nets. They looked like big net bags and had a drawstring opening at the top. The hay from the bale needed to be stuffed inside so that the horses could eat from it.

She opened the hay net up as far as she could and holding it in one hand, started pulling handfuls of hay from the bale with the other. But it was hard to stuff it inside the opening. Every time she tried, the hay net swung away from her.

Zoe could feel the frustration rising up inside her. *Just keep going*, she told herself. Every handful got a few more strands into the net.

I'm going to do this, even if it takes me all day! she thought to herself. Then she had a brainwave. She used one of her crutches to pin the hay net to the floor, then used her other hand to stuff the hay in. When Jack and Asha came back, she was hot and flustered, but the first net was almost full.

She grinned at them, but then sighed. There were still two more to do! 'It's … it's quite hard,' she admitted.

'We'll finish off for you,' said Jack cheerfully.

'Thanks.' Zoe watched as Jack and Asha finished filling the hay nets in less than a minute. Shutting her eyes, she took a deep breath, hating the fact her leg made everything so difficult. But she turned to Asha and gave a bright smile. 'What next?' she said.

Chapter Seven

Asha chattered about the guinea pigs non-stop as she and Zoe went over to clean them out. Bubble was chewing one of the new cardboard tubes in their day run, while Squeak was exploring the platforms and tunnels.

'It's much better for them now they've got lots to do,' said Asha, as Squeak scampered out of a tube and began to try and chew the rope ball. She grinned. 'Although it does mean two runs for us to clean out now!' She stepped into the run and picked up Bubble, giving him a kiss on his twitching nose. 'Lucky I love you so much!' she told him.

She put him down again and fetched a dustpan and brush from the side. Then she hesitated. Zoe realized the problem too. To clean out the guinea pig runs you had to kneel down and she simply couldn't kneel with her poorly leg.

'I'll just sit here for a moment,' she said, not wanting Asha to feel awkward. 'I don't mind. This way I get out of clearing up the guinea pig poo!' She acted like she was joking, but inside she felt a twist of sadness as she sat down on one of the benches. Staying positive was more difficult than Asha made it look!

'I'll be quick as I can and then we can do something else.' Asha crouched down and started to sweep up the droppings. Squeak ran over and started chasing the brush. 'Squeak!' giggled Asha as she tried to chew it. 'Here, I know what you can do, Zoe, you could hold her for me,' she said. 'It'll be much easier for me if she's out of the way.'

'Sure,' said Zoe. *At least I can manage to do that*, she added in her head.

Asha handed Squeak to her. 'Be careful, she is quite wriggly,' she warned. 'We usually only pick her up if we're in the pen.'

'I'll be careful,' Zoe promised.

Squeak crouched on Zoe's lap, her whiskers twitching, her bright eyes darting around. Zoe stroked her soft fur. 'You're beautiful, aren't you?' she murmured to her.

Squeak sat up taller. But then suddenly she was off! Zoe tried to grab her, but her hands caught thin air. She leaped off her lap onto the ground, running as fast as her little legs could take her.

Zoe tried to struggle to her feet, but her crutches were on the floor and her injured leg wouldn't take her weight. 'Asha!' she gasped, as Squeak scurried across the floor and hid under one of the other benches.

Asha moved like lightning. She flew to the door and bolted it shut, then she flung herself down on her hands and knees. 'Don't worry!' she called, peering under the bench. 'She's fine. I'll get her!'

Zoe sank helplessly down as Asha tempted the guinea pig out with a carrot. Within a couple of minutes he was nestling safely in Asha's arms again.

'He does move quickly,' said Asha. 'Maybe I should just keep him in the run like we're supposed to.'

Zoe nodded, her cheeks bright red with embarrassment. She couldn't even manage to hold a guinea pig! *I really can't do anything*, she thought miserably. She felt as if a grey cloud had fallen over her. *Who was I kidding when I thought I could be useful here? OK, I can groom a horse. But that's it. Big deal.*

Asha placed Squeak safely in the run. 'Can you unlock the door in case people want to come in?'

Zoe hobbled to the door. She felt the urge to get out of there. 'I ... I feel like some fresh air. I think I'll just go and check on Swift again.'

'Are you OK?' Asha asked.

Zoe forced a smile. 'Yeah ... yeah, I'm fine.' She hobbled out of the barn and out towards the field. She concentrated on her crutches, on moving them over the uneven ground, but inside she felt like crying. She wanted to help so much and yet all she did was cause trouble!

Swift was still pacing up and down by the gate. He stopped when he saw Zoe though, his gingery-brown ears pricking.

Putting her arms around his neck, Zoe buried her face in the base of his mane. Tears prickled at her eyes. 'Oh, Swift, I hate this! I want to be back like I was. I want to be able to run and move and do things without these stupid crutches! I hate not being able to do things and just having to watch.'

Swift nuzzled her shoulder. For a few moments, Zoe gave in to the tears but then she took a deep breath. Crying never helped with anything. She rubbed her tears away. Taking a breath she straightened up and looked at Swift. 'You're not happy either, are you, boy?'

She just couldn't work out what was the matter with him. He had everything he could want – a big stable, food, a field, company. He didn't have to do anything at all…

'Oh,' she breathed as she realized something. Maybe *that* was the problem. Swift might be too old to be a proper racehorse now, but he wasn't so old that he wanted to just stand in a field. She thought about how excited he had seemed when Rory had led him out of his stable and how disappointed he had looked to be turned out. He didn't just want to stand around any more than she wanted to sit and watch Jack and Asha do all the jobs around the farm.

'Is that it?' She stroked his cheek. 'You want to be out *doing* something?'

Swift gave her a sad look.

Zoe wondered what she could do to help. For a moment she pictured Bubble and Squeak exploring their new run. It was a pity they couldn't build Swift a play area to keep him busy! She looked around and her eyes fell on a neighbouring paddock. It was small and flat and had some old showjumping poles and barrels in. She remembered reading a chapter on training a young horse in Kerry's book. It had said how important groundwork was when training a young horse and suggested putting poles on the ground in a kind of maze and getting the horse to walk through it. It was supposed to make the horse think and become obedient. Swift might be well trained already but he still might enjoy it.

Excitement flooded through her, chasing her own unhappiness away. Maybe she could make him some sort of play area ... a special horse one!

Rory was filling the feed bins in the middle stable when Zoe found him. He listened to her idea and to her delight nodded approvingly. 'I think you could be on to something, lass. A horse like Swift isn't used to being idle. If you can think of ways to get him out and using his brain and exercising his legs then you go for it. We'll see how he reacts. Why don't you start setting things up and get Kerry when you're ready. She's our horse expert.'

'Brilliant! Thanks, Rory!' Zoe beamed.

Ten minutes later she was in the small paddock hobbling on her crutches and dragging the poles across the grass. She had forgotten all about being useless. *I can help Swift!* she thought, as she laid them out in a rectangular grid.

By the time she had finished there was a row of barrels to lead Swift through and a grid of poles on the ground. Zoe looked at the maze in satisfaction, then she hobbled over to get Kerry. 'Well, that sounds a great idea,' Kerry said approvingly when Zoe explained.

They went up to Swift's field together to bring him in. He was still standing at the gate. He looked at Zoe hopefully as she clipped the lead rope on.

'Are you happy leading him or would you like me to?' Kerry asked.

'Can I try?' Zoe asked.

Kerry smiled. 'Of course.' She held open the gate and Zoe led Swift out, holding the lead rein across the top of her crutches.

As they set off down the path towards the paddock with the poles and barrels in, she felt a moment's worry as Swift walked forward. What if he pulled her over? He was so big and strong. But Swift seemed to understand that she couldn't go very fast and slowed down so he was walking carefully beside her, adjusting his pace to hers.

Zoe led him into the little paddock. He stopped and looked warily at the poles and barrels.

'Keep talking to him and reassuring him,' said Kerry, shutting the gate. 'He'll look to you for leadership. Horses might be big but they like to be told what to do. You need to be calm and in control at all times.'

Zoe nodded. 'It's all right,' she murmured to Swift. 'There's nothing to be scared of. This is going to be fun.' Moving round to the front of him, she stroked his cheek and forehead.

'I'd start by leading him round and letting him have a look at everything first,' Kerry said. 'Then try moving him through the obstacles.'

Zoe did as she said, pointing the barrels and the poles out to Swift. 'Should I try the grid now?' she asked when he seemed calm.

'Sure,' Kerry called from the gate. 'But take it very slowly. I don't want you getting knocked over.'

Zoe nodded, but she had a feeling that Swift wouldn't hurt her in any way. He moved very carefully around her, his eyes watching her at all times. 'Here goes, boy,' she said, leading him towards the grid of poles. It was difficult to lead him through the grid with her crutches. The turns were tight and every few strides Zoe had to stop to adjust her position or back Swift up a pace or two. He didn't seem to understand at first what she wanted and trod on the poles or tried to step over them, rather than walking in and out of them. But hard though it was, Zoe didn't give up. She kept on going, working patiently, until he got the idea.

Soon Swift was stopping when she stopped, moving backwards at the lightest touch on his chest or shifting his body sideways slightly if she pressed his neck or side. Zoe felt a thrill run through her. He was listening to her, understanding her, trying to do what she wanted. What's more, he looked really happy – his eyes were shining and his ears were pricked as he worked.

'Good boy,' she praised, when they finally stopped.

Kerry climbed over the gate. 'That was fantastic, Zoe. It's clear how much he trusts you already. You're obviously developing a real bond with him.'

Zoe grinned from ear to ear.

'He's probably done enough for today now,' Kerry went on. 'Why don't we turn him back out in the field?'

Zoe led Swift to his turnout field. She was tired and her muscles were aching from doing so much but she felt very happy.

When she undid his head collar, Swift trotted off, sank down and rolled onto his side. 'What's he doing?' Zoe asked Kerry in surprise as the chestnut horse kicked his legs in the air.

'Enjoying himself.' Kerry smiled. 'Horses roll to groom themselves, and when they're feeling happy and relaxed.'

Rory joined them. 'Well, he certainly looks much happier. You were right, lass. He just needed something to do. Look at him go!' he added with a chuckle as Swift trotted in a circle round Stanley, his head high, his tail up. 'He's like a different horse!'

Zoe watched Swift trotting around so easily and lightly. 'I wish I could move like him,' she said, shifting her weight on her crutches.

Rory glanced at her. 'Maybe you'll be able to one day, lass.'

Zoe shook her head. 'Even when my cast comes off I'm always going to have a limp. I'm never going to be able to run around again.'

'Never say never,' Rory said. 'People often surprise themselves, that's what I always say.'

Swift stopped beside Stanley and looked towards them, his ears pricked.

Meeting his gaze, Zoe smiled.

Chapter Eight

The whole next week at school, Zoe daydreamed about City Farm. On Saturday morning she got up and dressed as quickly as she could. By the time she got into the car she was bursting with excitement. 'I can't wait to get there!' she squealed.

'I can tell,' Mum replied. 'You really are enjoying it, aren't you?'

'Oh yes!' Zoe sighed. 'It's brilliant! I'm going to do more with Swift today – and help tidy up the tack room and feed store.'

'All right, but don't do too much,' Mum warned. 'Remember you're supposed to be taking it easy.'

'I'm fine, Mum.' Zoe rolled her eyes.

Mum glanced across at her. 'Don't give me that look. I worry about you doing too much – I know what you're like, Zoe. You throw yourself into things, you always have done, but you've been in a serious accident. You *must* be careful.'

'I will.'

'No, I mean it. Zoe. Please take it easy.' Her mum swallowed. 'I just couldn't bear it if you hurt yourself again.'

Zoe sighed. Now that she was feeling so much better, she hated her mum fussing over her all the time.

'I'm sorry,' Mum said, seeing her face. 'I know I'm being overprotective and I'm sure I'll feel a bit more relaxed when your leg's out of plaster. But just for now – be careful. OK?'

'OK.'

Zoe was glad to get out of the car. She didn't want to be treated like an invalid any more. She remembered what Asha had said that first day, '*I don't want to go around letting myself feel sick and tired.*' She felt the same now.

'Morning!' Rory greeted her. 'Swift's looking out for you. Can you groom him?'

'Sure!' Zoe said eagerly.

'Kerry's going to have a word with you later. We've got a plan of how we can help keep Swift occupied and it involves you.'

'What is it?' asked Zoe curiously.

Rory tapped his nose. 'Aha.'

He walked into the barn. Zoe frowned. She wondered what the plan was. Oh well, as long as it involved her and Swift it *had* to be good!

Swift was looking over his stable door. As he saw her coming he whinnied. Zoe felt happiness rush through her. Reaching him, she put her arms around him. 'We're going to have a really good day today,' she promised.

Zoe groomed Swift until his coat gleamed. Afterwards, she led him out to the paddock and repeated everything she'd done the weekend before. Swift went through the maze perfectly, walking carefully, stopping and backing up straightaway when asked.

'He's looking good.' Zoe looked round and saw Kerry standing at the gate. 'I thought I'd come up and see how you were getting on,' Kerry said.

'He's remembered everything from last week,' said Zoe happily.

'I thought he might,' said Kerry. 'Thoroughbreds like Swift are very intelligent. The only problem is that means you'll soon run out of things to do on the ground with him to keep his brain active.'

Zoe felt worried. 'What will we do then?'

'Well,' Kerry said, 'I've had an idea. Wait here. I'll just fetch a few things.'

Zoe patted Swift, feeling intrigued. What was Kerry going to get? She stroked Swift's forehead and ears.

A few minutes later, Kerry came back. Zoe blinked. Kerry was carrying a saddle, bridle and a couple of riding helmets.

'You're going to ride him!' Zoe exclaimed.

Kerry put the saddle over the top bar of the fence. 'Not just me,' she said, raising her eyebrows. 'You too.'

Zoe's mouth dropped open. 'Me! I can't ride! What about my leg?'

'What about it?' said Kerry. 'I'm a qualified riding instructor, and I used to help out at a riding school that did lessons for disabled children. They had all sorts of problems, but they could all ride. You've just got an injured leg.'

Zoe looked at Swift, her head swirling at the thought of riding him. 'I ... I can't!'

'I think you can,' said Kerry. 'Swift's been retrained to have children riding him, so he should be fine. Besides, he loves you! I'll ride him first to check he's all right and then lead you round on him. We'll take it really slowly and really carefully, OK?'

'OK,' said Zoe. Excitement rushed through her. She had never imagined riding Swift herself. It would be amazing!

Kerry tacked Swift up, explaining to Zoe how all the straps did up and how important it was that the saddlecloth didn't have any creases in it and the girth that went under his stomach to hold the saddle on was comfortable. 'Always run your hand between the girth and his tummy,' said Kerry. 'Make sure there are no bits of skin being pinched. Now, let's try the helmets on. You've got to wear one that fits properly.'

The first helmet was too small, but the second fit Zoe perfectly. She waited by the gate while Kerry rode Swift round the field. He walked out, his stride swinging. He had his ears pricked and he looked as if he liked being ridden. After Kerry had trotted and cantered him she brought him back and dismounted. 'He's fine. So now it's your turn. I'll get Rory to come and help you get on – that's going to be the only tricky part, I think.'

Kerry called Rory and by the time she had checked Zoe's hat again, Rory was striding up to the gate, a bale of straw in his hands.

'So, what do you think of our plan, lass?' he boomed.

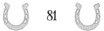

'I ... I like it!' said Zoe. She felt very excited but slightly nervous too.

'I thought you could use this to help you get on,' said Rory. He placed the bale on the ground next to Swift and then took Zoe's crutches and lifted her so she was standing on top of the bale. She held onto the front of the saddle to balance.

Kerry came and stood beside her. 'Now we'll just take this slowly. If Swift starts getting lively then we'll give up on the idea for now, but I've been watching him and he's got such a bond with you I'm absolutely sure he'll be fine. Let's see if we can get you up.' She carefully helped Zoe lean over Swift's saddle, then lifted her injured leg up so she could slide it over Swift's back. It was hard and the plaster cast was heavy, but Zoe was determined to do it. She managed to get her leg over the saddle and eased herself down into it.

'Perfect,' said Kerry. 'Just let your legs hang down. There's no point using stirrups – your foot won't fit in with the plaster cast on – but that's OK, you'll probably sit deeper in the saddle without them. That's a good thing when you're learning to ride. When I started, my riding teacher was always making me ride without stirrups.' She crossed the stirrups over the front of the saddle and took the reins from Rory, who left with a wave.

Zoe felt very high up and Swift's neck, from on top of him, seemed very long. The leg with her plaster cast on felt much heavier and she had to adjust her balance in the saddle to make up for it. But it was the most exciting thing that had happened to her since the accident. Swift's neck felt warm under her hands. She stroked his silky mane.

'Just pat him and get used to sitting there. You don't need to hold onto the reins – I've got him now and he's looking very calm,' said Kerry. Zoe stroked Swift's shoulder and then his neck. 'That's it. Now try twisting your body from side to side, just gently and slowly. If you're sitting nice and deep in the saddle it should be easy.'

Zoe did as she said and then Kerry got her circling her good ankle around and putting her hands on her head. 'Imagine you're a tree,' she told her. 'Your roots – that's the bottom half of your body – are reaching down into the ground. Your upper body is the branches, reaching into the sky.'

Zoe liked the image. As soon as she thought about it she immediately felt her position in the saddle shift. Her shoulders opened out and her head felt as if it was stretching taller while her legs felt as if they were reaching down towards the ground.

'That's great. Are you ready to try a walk?' asked Kerry.

Zoe nodded.

'Don't pick up the reins yet, but you can hold onto the strap around his neck – hold it if you feel unsteady.'

Zoe took hold of the neck strap and Kerry led Swift on. His stride was smooth and Zoe had no problem sitting to it. Soon she loosened her hold on the neck strap and relaxed into the saddle. She trusted Swift and didn't feel like she was going to fall off at all. It was lovely to be up so high and moving so smoothly. *And this is just walking*, she thought. *What would trotting or cantering be like?*

After a few times round, Kerry showed Zoe how to hold the reins and explained how to steer Swift – to go left she had to slightly pull on the left rein, and to turn right she had to pull the right rein. It all made sense. As Kerry explained it, Swift turned his head and nuzzled Zoe's uninjured leg with his nose. She smiled and patted him. She had the feeling he was trying to encourage her.

Soon Zoe was riding Swift with Kerry walking next to her but not holding onto her any more. She loved it. The slightest touch on the reins made Swift halt or turn. She tried very hard not to let her plaster cast bang against his side, concentrating on letting both legs hang softly next to him. It was brilliant getting about without having to use crutches. Now she understood what Rory had meant the day before when he had said that maybe she would be able to move around again easily!

After twenty minutes, Kerry stopped her. 'That'll do for now. You can have another ride on him this afternoon. But now I imagine he wants to go out and roll and have some grass, don't you, boy?'

Swift nodded his head to shake off a fly. Zoe giggled. 'I think he's saying yes!'

'I can't believe we didn't get to see you ride,' said Asha, as they all sat having their lunch.

'I'm going to ride him again later,' said Zoe. 'Why don't you ask if you could have a go?'

Asha shook her head. 'It's way too high up for me.'

Jack also shook his head. 'I love horses – but looking after them, not riding.'

Zoe felt a flicker of pleasure. If she was honest, she didn't want her friends riding Swift. She loved having something that only she could do.

'Maybe you'll get really good at riding,' Asha

85

said eagerly. 'And then instead of being an Olympic runner, you could be an Olympic rider!'

Zoe tensed, half waiting for the twist of pain which always came whenever she thought of never running in the Olympics. But to her surprise she didn't feel anything this time. Her mind was too full of riding Swift. She smiled at Asha. 'I'm not sure about riding in the Olympics. I've only had one riding lesson. I might not even turn out to be any good at riding.'

'I bet you will be!' said Asha optimistically.

'And the important thing is Swift will love you riding him, even if you're just learning,' said Jack practically. 'As your leg heals you'll be able to go faster. I bet he'll think that's great!'

Zoe smiled. Jack was right. Swift would love to be ridden and would be so much happier in his new life at City Farm – that was the most important thing by far!

At half past three, Zoe got Swift out again. This time she managed to put the saddle and bridle on by herself with Kerry watching. When she mounted, she felt much more confident. She took hold of the reins properly and rode him round, trying circles and halts and turning. It all felt so easy. She remembered what

Asha had said at lunch time and felt excitement grip her. It might only be her first day of riding him, but maybe Asha was right … maybe she could get to be really good…

'Can I go faster?' she asked Kerry.

'I don't see why you can't try a slow trot. I'll lead him and you can hold onto the front of the saddle,' said Kerry. 'We'll have a trot down the side of the field. Are you sitting deep and holding on?'

'Yep!' said Zoe.

Kerry clicked her tongue and Swift started to trot. Zoe hung on tight. It was very bumpy but she really liked it. It felt so fast, just like running with the wind on her face.

'Can we do it again?' she gasped as soon as Kerry slowed to a walk. Asha and Jack were grinning at her from the gate. Jack gave her a thumbs-up.

'One more time,' said Kerry, smiling.

'Zoe!' A horrified voice rang through the air.

Zoe swung round. 'Mum!' she gasped, seeing her mum running to the gate.

'What *are* you doing?' her mum demanded. She pulled the gate open. Her face was pale. Zoe's heart sank. 'Get off that horse at once!'

'Mrs Clarke, it's all right,' Kerry said in a calm

voice. 'Zoe's doing incredibly well.'

Zoe's mum's voice shook. 'She shouldn't be riding at all! What if she falls off and injures herself? She's been hurt enough already! Zoe, get down now!'

Zoe looked at Kerry, who nodded. Zoe lifted her leg awkwardly over the saddle and slid off, holding onto Swift's saddle for support. 'Mum, please don't make a scene,' she pleaded.

'A scene! I think I'm more than justified in making a scene!' Mum turned on Kerry. 'How could you be so irresponsible? I thought Harvest Hope was supposed to be a safe place for Zoe to come. It appears I was wrong!'

'Now, Mrs Clarke—' Kerry began.

Zoe's mum didn't listen. 'Zoe, you're coming home right now and you are *not* coming back!' she interrupted.

'What!' Zoe gasped in horror.

'No, I'm not prepared to have you put in danger.' Mum fetched Zoe's crutches and handed them to her. 'Get in the car!'

Chapter Nine

'Mum! You can't stop me going to City Farm!' Zoe stared desperately at her mum as she drove quickly out of the car park. 'I'm friends with everyone there and I've been having a really good time. Isn't that what you wanted?'

'Yes, but what I didn't expect was that they would put you in danger!' Mum snapped.

'I wasn't in danger! Kerry made sure it was safe – she was with me the whole time. And Swift was brilliant, he was really calm.'

'Zoe, you shouldn't have been riding at all!' Mum ran a hand through her hair. 'I'm sorry. I know you like it there, but I can't let you go if they're going to be so irresponsible with your wellbeing.'

'They're not irresponsible!' Zoe cried. '*Mum!*'

'No, Zoe,' her mum said firmly. 'I don't want to hear another word.'

Zoe slumped back against the seat, feeling tears welling up. She tried to swallow them but they trickled down her cheeks. A sob burst out of her.

Her mum looked over at her and then touched her arm. 'Zoe…' she said more softly.

Zoe shook her off. 'You don't understand!' she cried. She couldn't bear the thought of not going to City Farm again, of not seeing her friends and, most of all, not seeing Swift again.

Her mum sighed. She didn't say anything more and they drove the rest of the way home in silence.

When Zoe got out of the car she went straight to her bedroom. She threw herself down on the bed and gave way to tears. To think, that afternoon she had been feeling so happy.

'It's not fair!' she sobbed.

She'd already had her life ruined once by the accident and now, just when it was starting to look like it might be OK after all, it had all been torn apart again.

No more Swift. No more Asha and Jack, no more Kerry and Rory. No more City Farm.

Zoe cried until all her tears were gone. Then she

just lay there making the occasional sob, feeling the tears dry to sticky tracks on her cheeks.

There was a gentle knock on the door. 'Zoe, love?' she heard her mum's voice.

'Leave me alone!' Zoe said.

'But Zoe—'

'I don't want to talk to you!'

Mum paused, but Zoe didn't hear her walk away. 'It was just so scary seeing you in hospital,' Mum said in a little voice. 'I love you so much, Zoe, and I couldn't bear it if you got hurt again.' There was a long pause. 'Your dinner's waiting,' Mum said eventually. 'Come along when you're ready.'

Zoe's heart sank as she heard Mum's footsteps going away. It was horrible that her mum was upset, but it was worse that she couldn't see Swift or do anything that she loved. She might as well just sit inside all day long.

Rolling onto her back, Zoe took a deep breath and tried to calm herself down.

Maybe Mum would change her mind. Maybe in the morning everything would be different…

In the morning, Zoe's eyes were sore and puffy. She was really hungry too, but her tummy still twisted when she thought about Swift. She *couldn't* stop going to City Farm. She had to change her mum's mind. Even if she couldn't ride Swift again, she still wanted to be able to look after him and see her friends. *I'll talk to Mum*, she thought. *Make her listen…*

She was just getting out of bed when Mum knocked on the door and came in with some breakfast on a tray.

'You must be hungry,' her mum said, putting the tray down on her desk.

'Have you changed your mind?' Zoe blurted out.

'No, Zoe—' Mum started.

Zoe swung her bad leg out of bed crossly. Just then the doorbell rang.

'I wonder who that could be?' Mum said, rushing to the door.

Zoe ignored her and started pulling on her clothes. There was the sound of the door opening and voices – a woman's voice and a girl's voice. Zoe frowned and listened as she got dressed.

'Please don't stop Zoe coming to City Farm!' the girl was saying. 'We'll miss her!' It was Asha. Asha and Kerry!

'I'm really sorry about what happened, Mrs Clarke,' Zoe heard Kerry say. 'I would never have let

Zoe ride Swift if I'd known you would have a problem with it. Please can she come back – she has fitted in so well and I'm sure it was doing her good being on the farm.'

Zoe heard her mum sigh. 'I have to agree with you. She's been like a different girl the last two weeks – almost back to her old happy self. I don't know. I've been thinking about it – I never expected her to be so upset. Maybe I *have* been too hasty.' Zoe's breath caught in her throat, her heart lifting. 'Look, let me get her and we can talk this through.'

Zoe pulled her jumper over her head and hobbled to her bedroom door, opening it before Mum even had time to knock. Her mum looked at her anxiously.

'Zoe, Kerry and Asha are—'

'I know,' Zoe interrupted. She saw Kerry and Asha waiting in the corridor. 'I heard what you were saying. Oh, please can I go back to City Farm, Mum?'

'All right,' said her mum reluctantly. 'But you're not to ride,' she added.

Zoe nodded quickly and Mum gave her a big hug. She'd agree to anything if only her mum would let her still keep going to the farm. 'All right,' she murmured into Mum's shoulder. 'That's fine.' She felt a stab of sorrow, but she pushed it away. The important thing was still being able to see Swift – and her friends.

'I'm sorry,' her mum said softly. 'But your leg is very fragile still. Just imagine if you fell off. Will you promise me you won't ride again?'

'I promise,' Zoe agreed.

'I'll make sure she doesn't,' said Kerry.

'Thank you.' Mrs Clarke gave Kerry an apologetic look. 'I guess you must think I'm horribly overprotective.'

'It's all right. I do understand,' said Kerry gently. 'You've all been through a dreadful ordeal and you just want to keep Zoe safe.'

Mrs Clarke nodded. 'Yes. Would you like to come through for a coffee, Kerry?'

'That would be lovely. Thank you,' Kerry said.

While Kerry went into the kitchen, Asha came into Zoe's room. 'I'm so glad you're going to be able to come back to City Farm,' she said, shutting the door. 'Your mum really freaked when she saw you riding Swift, didn't she?'

'Totally,' said Zoe, tucking into her breakfast hungrily. 'But at least I'm not banned from coming back now.' She breathed a sigh of relief. 'I'm so glad!'

'Me too!' said Asha. She looked round at Zoe's room at all the unpacked boxes. 'Did you just move in? This is a nice room.'

'No,' Zoe shrugged. 'I had to move down here after the accident. I prefer my old room though. Do you want to see it?'

'Sure.' Asha grinned.

Zoe took her crutches and they went to the staircase.

'Do you want a hand?' Asha said.

'I think I can do it, if you can just take one crutch for me,' said Zoe. She used the other banister and crutch to get up the staircase. It was slow, but she felt a rush of triumph when they reached the top. It was the first time she'd been upstairs since the accident. Asha gave her the other crutch and Zoe led the way into her old bedroom. It was a big light room with a window seat looking out over the garden. It hadn't really changed – her old bed was there, her blue curtains with stars on, white wardrobe and desk, and the walls covered with running posters. The shelves were full of the trophies and medals from races she'd won. Zoe sighed. She wished it was still her bedroom.

'This is a lovely room too,' said Asha, going to the window. 'You can hear the birds singing – and look, there's a squirrel in the tree over there! He's so cute.'

Zoe joined her and saw the squirrel scampering up the trunk. 'I used to watch the squirrels loads,' she said. She watched him for a moment and then looked around the room again. 'It's strange looking at these now.' She pointed to the posters.

Asha sat down on the bed. 'Maybe when your plaster cast is off you'll be able to move back up here.'

'Maybe,' Zoe said. 'But I don't want the posters. They just remind me of what I can't do – of the dreams I had.'

'But you can have new dreams,' Asha said positively. 'You can get new posters.'

Zoe shook her head.

'Of course you can,' insisted Asha.

Zoe shrugged. 'Maybe.' But she didn't mean it. She didn't want ever to have any dreams again. It just hurt too much when they were shattered. Her Olympic running dream had gone – and now even her smaller dream of one day being able to trot and canter Swift had gone too. *No dreams*, she thought. *Not any more.* She changed the subject. 'Hey. Do you like music? My CD player is still in here. We could put a CD on if you don't mind fetching one from my desk downstairs?'

'Sure,' said Asha cheerfully, leaping to her feet.

She came back with a selection and then they listened to music and talked about their schools until Kerry had finished her coffee.

'I'd better take you back to the farm, Asha.' Kerry glanced between Zoe and Mum. 'You'd better have the day off today, Zoe, but we'll see you next weekend,' she said. 'I'll look after Swift for you until then.'

'Thanks,' said Zoe with a smile.

'We'll have to think of something else for him to do now you're not going to be riding him, so get your thinking cap on.'

'And next Saturday you'll get to meet Emily,' said Asha to Zoe. 'She used to be on the Harvest Hope project and she's really fun. And her dog, Patch, is gorgeous.'

Zoe waved them off.

'So, are you OK?' Mum asked as they shut the door.

Zoe nodded.

'I shouldn't have overreacted as I did. I'm sorry. I was just really worried. I do want you to be happy, Zoe.'

Then let me ride, Zoe wanted to say, but she bit the words back. She didn't want her mum changing her mind and deciding not to let her go back after all. She sighed. 'I … I think I'm going to go and have a rest,' she said.

'All right, poppet.' Her mum kissed her.

Zoe hobbled to her new room and went inside.

Leaning against the door she shut her eyes and thought about Swift. So she couldn't ride him, but at least she could see him. *Just be happy with that*, she thought.

Chapter Ten

A week later, Zoe grinned as she hurried up to Swift's stable as fast as she could on her crutches. Swift was looking over his door. He whinnied when he saw her. She put her arms round his neck and he snuffled at her face and blew on her hair. Zoe hugged him tightly. 'I've missed you so much, Swift!'

His chestnut coat was muddy from all the rolling he had been doing in the field. 'I'll go and get your grooming kit and make you look beautiful,' she said.

Soon she was busy grooming him. The others arrived – and so did Emily Keane. She was eleven like Zoe. Her silvery-grey dog, Patch, was beautiful, even though she seemed a little nervous of everyone apart from Emily. She rarely left Emily's side.

'I'm glad you've settled in so quickly,' Emily said,

as she and Asha and Jack mucked out the stable while Zoe groomed Swift. 'I was horrible when I first came. I didn't really mean to be but I was so upset by stuff that was going on at home that I just ended up being really cross with everyone here.'

'Jack and I thought you hated us,' remembered Asha.

Emily stroked Patch and looked shame-faced. 'I know. I didn't mean half of the things I said. Luckily Patch came along and things started to get better.'

The collie licked her nose.

'I was horrible when I arrived too,' Jack said quickly.

Zoe couldn't imagine Jack being anything other than cheerful and friendly. 'Really?'

Jack nodded. 'I thought this place was stupid because it was so small after my grandad's farm,' he went on. 'But being here has been great.'

'City Farm's wonderful, isn't it?' said Asha happily. 'I think it would make anyone feel better.'

Zoe laid her head against Swift's broad side. It was certainly helping her. 'Uh-oh,' Jack sighed. 'There's the one person who doesn't think City Farm's wonderful!'

Zoe looked out into the farmyard to see Rory and Kerry rushing along behind a small man in a suit. His grey hair was slicked down and he was peering at a clipboard. 'I know I haven't made an appointment, Mr Trent,' he was saying in a whiny voice. 'But article 73A in the council's administration document clearly states that if there is room for concern then the council may do a spot check. I would like to conduct an inspection.'

Zoe and the others exchanged worried looks and went to the door.

'It's Derrick Jarvis, from the council,' hissed Asha to Zoe.

Zoe remembered the name. It was the person Kerry had been talking to on the phone the other day. He was the one who Asha had said wanted to shut City Farm. She gave him a look of dislike.

'Well, look around all you like,' said Rory.

'Oh dear.' Mr Jarvis shook his head as he looked at the stable roof patched with the tarpaulin sheet. 'Oh dear, oh dear, I don't like the look of that at all. Could you fetch me a ladder, Mr Trent?'

It was funny hearing Rory being called Mr Trent. He exchanged exasperated looks with Kerry and then went to get a ladder from the store. Mr Jarvis climbed up a few rungs. He peered unhappily at the tarpaulin and lifted up a corner. 'We can't have this,' he said, tut-tutting. 'The tiles are loose. Once the weather gets rough they could dislodge and fall on someone's head.'

'It'll do for now,' said Kerry. 'I promise you we'll get it fixed up soon.'

Mr Jarvis came down the ladder. 'Soon is not good enough, Miss Barker. This can't wait. It's a health and safety issue.'

'But it's been like this for ages,' said Rory practically. 'And nothing's happened to anyone.'

'That's as may be, but I'm afraid I can't ignore it. You're going to have to get it fixed straightaway.'

'But we haven't got the money,' protested Kerry. 'Roofs are expensive to repair.'

'Well, I would advise you to *find* the money, Miss Barker,' said Mr Jarvis, his voice clipped. 'Otherwise there are two options: one, you can move the horses out of this stable block and cordon it off so no one can come near it—'

'We can't move the horses out!' Rory exclaimed. 'There isn't another stable big enough for Swift – he's an ex-racehorse.'

'What's the second option?' Kerry said grimly.

'Or two,' – Mr Jarvis gave a toothy grin – 'City Farm shuts down.'

'No!' gasped Asha.

Derrick Jarvis ignored her. 'Oh dear,' he said,

twirling his pen. 'If the racehorse can't move then you will obviously have to get rid of it. I'm not sure what an animal like that is doing here anyway. This is supposed to be a farm, not a racetrack! So,' he cleared his throat, 'I shall give you until a week on Monday to find a solution.' He turned on his heels and strode away in his shiny shoes, dodging carefully round the puddles.

There was a moment's silence and then everyone spoke at once.

'Rory!' Zoe exclaimed. 'What are we going to do?'

'He can't make us get rid of Swift!' said Asha.

'No way!' said Emily.

'The council can make the farm do anything it wants,' said Jack to Kerry, 'can't it?'

She nodded. 'Unfortunately they really can stop us from using the stable block.'

'Aye, lad.' Rory rubbed his head anxiously. 'And we can't keep Swift anywhere but here, so heaven knows what we're going to do!'

Kerry called an emergency meeting in the barn. They all squashed in on the sofas. There was a tray of drinks and chocolate brownies from the café. But for once no one seemed to feel like eating or drinking.

'This is all very serious,' Kerry said, twisting the end of a braid round one of her fingers. 'You all heard what Mr Jarvis said. If we can't raise the money to mend the roof then we'll have to stop using the stables.'

'We can try and raise the money though, can't we?' said Zoe. 'We used to have lots of fundraisers at my old athletics club.'

Kerry nodded. 'We can certainly try. Has anyone got any bright ideas? It's got to be something we can do quickly. We've only got until a week Monday to come up with the money.'

'Could we sell cakes in the café?' suggested Zoe.

'We could, but the café already does that,' said Kerry, 'and the money we get from it is needed to feed the animals. But if we got extra visitors in we'd sell more cakes – how can we get extra visitors in though?'

They all thought hard.

'A display!' Asha exclaimed. 'How about…' She looked around, thinking, and her eyes fell on Jack. 'How about Jack does a talk about Cynthia and shows off her footballing skills? I'm sure people would come and see a footballing pig!'

'I could definitely do that,' said Jack eagerly.

'Great,' said Kerry, making a note on a pad she was

holding. 'Any other ideas?'

"Maybe we could knit some things,' Asha said, seeing a woolly scarf of Kerry's hanging on the back of the door. 'Though I can't knit. Or … or…'

Rory shook his head. 'If we could raise money by you talking, lass, we'd save the stables in no time!'

Asha sighed. 'I don't think anyone's going to pay me to talk.'

'Maybe to stop talking,' said Jack.

'That's it!' Asha cried, jumping to her feet. 'I could do a sponsored silence for a whole day!'

They all stared at her.

'Asha!' Emily said. 'You'd never manage to be quiet for a whole day!'

'I would if it was to help Swift!' said Asha. 'I'll do it!'

'Right, well I'm not going to say no. So, that's Asha down for a sponsored silence,' said Kerry, making another quick note. 'Any other ideas?'

Emily stroked Patch. 'How about we offer to groom people's pets?'

'We could turn the farmhouse into a grooming parlour!' said Asha enthusiastically.

Rory's bushy eyebrows raised. 'My farmhouse, you mean?'

Asha smiled sweetly at him. 'Yes, but you wouldn't mind, would you, Rory? It would be for a *very* good cause.'

Rory gave a chuckle. 'Oh, all right then.' He sighed. 'I must be mad!'

Asha beamed.

'I'll organize it,' put in Emily eagerly. 'I love grooming cats and dogs.'

'And I'll help!' said Asha.

Kerry added *grooming parlour* to the list.

Zoe wracked her brains. She really wanted to make a good suggestion too. But what? Her eyes fell on a photo by Kerry's desk. It was of Kerry riding a horse. She remembered how wonderful it had felt to be riding Swift. 'Could we give rides to people and charge them? Or maybe not just rides,' she said, thinking of the pony rides she had been on when she was younger. It had always been kind of boring, just walking once round a field. 'How about you give lessons – just short ones on Swift? Maybe fifteen minutes. We could use Stanley too.'

'That's not a bad idea, you know,' said Kerry thoughtfully. 'Stanley's too old to be ridden regularly, but he'd be fine just for one day if we only let very small children on him. It's a shame Dusty's too grumpy to give rides. As for Swift…' She weighed it up in her mind. 'It would be good to stop him getting bored. OK, we'll do it. You can be my assistant horse-riding teacher, Zoe, and organize the riding hat fittings and take people's money. So, I think with all these ideas we should have a big fundraising day next Sunday. All those in favour?'

Everyone raised their hands.

'Great!' declared Kerry, her eyes shining. 'We must get some posters up advertising it.'

'I'll do them!' offered Zoe. 'I'll put on about the horse rides.'

'And Cynthia, and the grooming service,' Asha said.

'Not just a grooming service, but "The Pampered Pets' Parlour"!' declared Emily.

'And not just riding lessons, but "Harvest Hope Horse Rides"!' grinned Zoe.

'Oh, this is perfect!' said Asha, clapping her hands together. 'We're going to raise loads of money. I just know it!' She looked at the tray of chocolate brownies. 'I feel much hungrier now.'

'Then let's tuck in,' said Kerry. She handed round the brownies and drinks.

Rory lifted his glass. 'Here's to raising enough

money to repair the stables!'

They all clinked glasses. 'To our fundraising!' said Kerry.

'To saving Swift,' Zoe whispered.

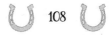

Chapter Eleven

All week Zoe told everyone she met about the City Farm fundraiser. She hoped lots of them would come and give them enough money for the new roof.

She rang Kerry on Wednesday to see how Swift was. 'I think he's missing you,' said Kerry. 'I've ridden him and given him a quick brush most days, but it's so hard finding the time. I'll be glad at the weekend when you can take over again and give him the attention he needs.'

Zoe wished she could see Swift every day. She was longing for it to be the summer holidays, then she would be able to go to the farm and see him all the time. *If we raise enough money to repair the stable block, that is,* she reminded herself. Icy fingers ran down her spine.

On Sunday morning everyone arrived early to start getting the animals ready for the big event. While Kerry and Rory brushed the farmyard and tidied everywhere up, Asha and Emily set to work converting one of the downstairs rooms in Rory's farmhouse into a pet grooming parlour. They put a table in there and hairdryers and washed and cleaned all the grooming tools the farm had, although it took them longer than it would have done because Asha had started her sponsored silence. It meant she couldn't say a word! If she wanted to tell anyone anything she had to write it down. It was very strange not to hear Asha's voice chattering all the time.

While Asha and Emily sorted out the grooming parlour, Jack helped Zoe get Stanley and Swift ready so they would look their best for the visitors when they arrived.

Zoe liked grooming with Jack. As they worked he told her about the horses that he had used to help look after on his grandad's farm. 'There was a pony called Smoky who my mum had learned to ride on, and a big chestnut horse called Mary who Grandad used to ride. They lived out in the field with the sheep most of the time. They had to be sold when Grandad moved out.' His voice faltered. 'I ... I really miss them.' He turned away.

Zoe bit her lip. 'I'm sorry.'

'It's OK.' Jack shrugged.

But Zoe knew it must have been awful for him. She stroked Swift's neck, imagining saying goodbye to *him*. Where would he go? Who would take him in? Would she ever see him again?

'So how's your leg doing?' Jack said, interrupting her horrible thoughts. 'You're not using your crutches. Are you getting better?'

With a start, Zoe realized that he was right. She'd put her crutches down while she groomed and now she was managing to stand next to Swift without balancing against him. 'I guess I am,' she said. She'd been so focused on grooming and on the fundraiser, she simply hadn't thought about her crutches or her leg. Hope flared through her. Maybe she *was* finally getting better.

'How much longer will you have the cast on for?' asked Jack curiously.

'Only a couple more weeks.' Zoe was slightly dreading seeing what her leg looked like. It would have a scar – the doctor had warned her about that. Still, it would be wonderful to have the cast off.

'You'll have to buy some new jeans,' Jack said.

'You mean, you don't think these look good? You're so uncool!' teased Zoe, pointing at the jean leg that was cut so it'd fit over her cast.

Jack laughed. 'Maybe you're right, maybe we should all wear jeans like that.'

'Yeah, especially Rory,' said Zoe. 'I can just see it – *not!*'

They both cracked up at the thought.

Zoe threw the grooming brush into the tray. 'Well, I think we're done with grooming now,' she said, looking at Swift and Stanley. Their coats were shining and their manes and tails hung in silken strands. 'What next?'

'Getting Cynthia ready for her big appearance, of course,' said Jack. 'Do you want to come and watch me bathe her? You could try and help but you might get knocked over – she gets very grumpy when anyone tries to wash her.'

'I think I'll just watch,' Zoe said with a laugh.

They headed down the yard and met Asha and Emily by the barn. Asha was looking very fed-up. 'Are you OK?' Zoe asked her.

Asha scribbled something on the pad she had taken to carrying round and held it up. It said: *I'm BORED of being quiet!*

'Think of all the money you're raising,' Zoe grinned. Almost everyone Asha knew had sponsored her. If she could last the full day she'd raise lots of money! Asha sighed and nodded.

The three girls hung over the gate of the pigsty while Jack tried to wash Cynthia with some warm water and a brush.

'She doesn't look like she likes it much!' called Zoe as Cynthia ran away from him and then rolled in the mud. As she got up she looked at Jack and grunted crossly.

'I'll have another go.' Jack headed towards the pig again. 'Come on, Cynthia.'

Cynthia charged at his legs. 'Whoa!' Jack yelled, leaping out of the way just in time but skidding on some pig poo. He landed on his bottom and dropped the bucket so the water splashed all over him.

Asha, Zoe and Emily burst out laughing.

'I thought Cynthia was supposed to be having the bath, not *you*!' said Zoe, as Emily and Asha climbed over the gate and ran to help him up.

Cynthia stopped at the far side of her pen and grunted again, her little black eyes gleaming. It sounded just like she was laughing too!

'I give up!' groaned Jack, as the girls hauled him to

his feet.

'Now, what's going on here?' a clipped voice said.

They turned and saw Derrick Jarvis approaching the sty with Kerry. He was looking very disapproving, his forehead furrowed in a frown as he surveyed the scene.

'What's he doing here?' Zoe hissed to Emily.

'He's doing another inspection,' she whispered back. 'Kerry told me and Asha earlier.'

Zoe watched as Mr Jarvis made a note on the clipboard he was carrying. 'This is most unacceptable. Children really should not be allowed in unsupervised with a dangerous creature like that.' He shot a look at Kerry.

Asha looked about to burst with indignation. Her eyes widened as she fought to keep her mouth closed.

'Oh, Cynthia's not dangerous,' said Kerry hastily.

'No way!' exclaimed Jack. 'Look.' He kicked the bucket away and crouched down. Cynthia gave a snort and then ambled over and butted her big head affectionately against Jack's chest.

'Hmm.' Mr Jarvis pursed his lips so his mouth almost disappeared, but even he couldn't deny that Cynthia looked friendly as she snuffled and snorted at Jack, pushing her nose against his cheek.

'You can try cuddling her too if you want,' Kerry offered the council officer. 'See just how friendly she is for yourself.'

The council officer's eyes widened in horror. 'Cuddle a pig? You certainly won't see me doing something so ridiculous!' He hastily backed away.

'It's fine,' said Jack. 'Really it is. She won't hurt you.' He got up and headed to the gate. 'Come on in.'

But Mr Jarvis was already hurrying back up the path as fast as his shiny shoes would carry him.

'I guess he didn't fancy the idea!' said Kerry, shaking her head.

Zoe stared after the man with dislike. She wished she could let Cynthia out to charge at him and butt him over!

'I'd better go after him,' said Kerry with a sigh. 'I don't know why he had to come on a Sunday. He seems determined to try and find a reason to shut us down.'

'Well, we're not going to let him,' declared Emily. 'We're going to make loads of money today and then he'll have to leave the farm alone!'

Zoe nodded, but felt very anxious. What if they didn't make the money they needed? What if Mr Jarvis got his way?

*

By ten o'clock Derrick Jarvis had gone and the yard and all the animals were spotless – except Cynthia, of course. Zoe went up to the stables. Swift whickered softly as she came towards him, his dark eyes lighting up. Zoe felt a rush of love. 'Oh, Swift, it's such an important day. I hope you're going to like giving rides.'

Swift snorted and nuzzled her hair. Zoe began to tack him up.

From the moment the gates opened, a steady stream of visitors arrived – some regulars and some new people. Soon the café was heaving and Daisy was doing a roaring trade.

Zoe had no idea how Emily and Asha were getting on, although she did see lots of people with cats in carriers and dogs on leads heading down the path to the farmhouse. Asha had hung the bunting she'd used to welcome Zoe and Swift the first day over the door, and put up a big sign saying: *Pampered Pets Here!*

Zoe was busy with the horses. As people arrived they could put their names down for a fifteen-minute riding lesson. Zoe wrote their names on a big chalkboard and took their money, then she fitted them with a riding helmet. Kerry had explained to her how to make sure the helmet wasn't so small it was sitting up high on someone's head, or so big it was coming down over their eyes. Rory had carried up some bales of straw so that people would have somewhere to sit while they waited.

The first customer was a little boy called Callum. He was much too small for Swift. Kerry led him round on Stanley and told him what to do.

Zoe waited with Swift. He looked round with interest at the people and the helmets and the chalkboard. 'You've got to be really good,' Zoe told him. He nuzzled her hopefully. She had a feeling he thought she was about to ride him. 'It's not me riding you,' she said with a flash of sadness. She would have loved to have been one of the people having a lesson on him. 'I'm just here to help today.'

'Excuse me.' A girl who was a bit younger than Zoe came over shyly. 'Please may I put my name down for a lesson?'

'Of course,' said Zoe, smiling at her. 'Do you want to ride Stanley – that's the pony being ridden now – or Swift?'

'Oh, I'd love to ride him!' said the girl pointing at Swift. 'He's beautiful.'

Zoe smiled. Swift was looking wonderful that day, the sun making his coat gleam.

'What's your name?'

'Natalie,' the girl said shyly.

Zoe wrote Natalie's name down on the board and then fitted her with a helmet. Soon it was Natalie's turn to have a lesson. Zoe untied Swift and Kerry came to help Natalie on. She stood on a straw bale so she could reach the stirrup and mounted.

'Have you ridden before?' Kerry asked her.

Natalie nodded as she adjusted the stirrups. 'I've been riding for a few years.' She patted Swift's neck. 'But I've never ridden a horse like Swift.' She took hold of the reins, gripping them tightly as Kerry adjusted her stirrups. Zoe saw Swift raise his head and nod it up and down. She could tell he didn't like having his mouth held so tightly.

'Maybe just hold your reins a bit looser,' she said. 'Swift's mouth is very sensitive.'

Natalie eased her fingers. Swift looked much happier and stopped tossing his head.

'Thanks,' Natalie said.

'Right,' Kerry said. 'When you're ready, walk on.'

Swift behaved beautifully, walking and trotting when she asked. As Zoe watched Natalie riding Swift round with Kerry beside her, she had to fight her jealousy. She wished she could be the one riding him.

She envied the way Natalie rose up and down lightly in the saddle – she wanted to be able to learn to ride like that. Zoe couldn't watch any more. She turned away and busied herself with checking Stanley's saddle and running a brush over his coat and through his tail again as he munched at his hay net.

She was just putting the brush away when she heard her mum's voice. 'Hi, Zoe!'

Zoe smiled. Her mum had told her she would pop in and support the fundraising.

'How's it going?' her mum said, coming to the fence.

'Really well,' said Zoe, glancing over to where Natalie was trotting Swift in a circle.

'Isn't Swift being good?' her mum said in surprise. 'That girl can't be more than about nine.'

'He is good. He's really calm and gentle considering he used to be a racehorse. His old owners weren't very nice, but they did retrain him well.'

'His coat's very glossy,' her mum said.

Zoe was pleased. 'I groomed him for ages!'

Her mum looked at her and shook her head. 'You know, I'm proud of you, Zoe Clarke. You've been amazing since the accident.'

Zoe blushed. 'Mum!' she said in her *you're-*

embarrassing-me voice.

Her mum smiled. 'Sorry, poppet. Right, I'll leave you to it and go and have a look around. I want to buy a cake for tea.'

Natalie halted and dismounted. 'He was *so* good! Thank you for teaching me,' she said to Kerry as she took her helmet off. 'I've learned lots!'

'You rode really well,' Kerry told her.

As Natalie ran off, Kerry led Swift over to Zoe. 'Well, I hope he's as good with everyone today,' she said.

'He will be!' Zoe declared.

But she spoke too soon. Swift was very good with anyone who was quiet and gentle, but he didn't seem to like it much when people pulled his mouth or wobbled in the saddle. Kerry was very patient, and as she explained what to do the people got better at riding, but Swift started to toss his head more. After the fifth person had got off him after their lesson ended, Kerry brought him over to Zoe. 'This won't work any longer. He's just too sensitive to be ridden by beginners.'

'But I'm a beginner and he was fine with me,' protested Zoe.

'You're special,' Kerry smiled. 'Swift loves you.

You're a natural in the saddle, you were relaxed and didn't hang on too tightly to his mouth,' she said. 'Most beginners tense up when a horse starts to move. It's not their fault but it's why thoroughbreds like Swift aren't usually used to teach riding. It's best to have a horse or pony who's quiet and slow. We can still carry on with the rides,' said Kerry. 'But only on Stanley, I think. I don't want Swift to get stressed. Will you take him in?'

Zoe led Swift back up to his stable. Swift had a long drink and rested his head against her chest. 'I wish I could ride you again,' she said longingly. 'We both liked that, didn't we?' She rested her forehead against his and shut her eyes, remembering the day she had ridden him. *Oh, if only I could have learned to ride really well. We could have cantered and galloped*, she thought. *Maybe even gone in for shows. It would have been amazing.* She shook her head. 'No more dreams,' she said out loud.

'Zoe?'

Zoe swung round and saw her mum looking over the door.

'Sorry, I didn't mean to startle you,' Mum said. 'I just stopped by to say goodbye.' She frowned. 'What do you mean, love? *No more dreams?*'

121

'It doesn't matter.'

'No, tell me,' her mum, said coming into the stable. Swift stepped towards her and sniffed at her hands. She stroked him. 'You've always had goals and dreams. Your leg might not work as well any more, but that's no reason to give up on having dreams.'

Zoe swallowed. 'I don't want to have them. It hurts too much when they end up in pieces.'

'But Zoe, you can't think like that!' her mum protested. 'It's only your running dream that has gone.'

'And my riding one! I might have only ridden Swift twice, but I wanted to try and be really good. Maybe go in for competitions. That's not going to happen now, is it? It's OK,' Zoe interrupted, seeing her mum about to speak. 'I get it. I know it's just 'cos you're worried about me and I don't want you to be worried and upset and I'm just glad I can still come here. But I'm through with having dreams!'

Swift nuzzled her. He could tell she was upset. Zoe braced herself, waiting for Mum to tell her off.

But Mum didn't say anything for a few minutes. And then, 'You love him very much, don't you?' she said softly.

Zoe nodded. She was silent for a moment and then

the words burst from her. 'Oh, Mum. What if he has to leave? What if we don't raise enough money today?'

Mum put an arm round her shoulders. 'Let's think positive. It looks like the fundraising day is going really well. There are loads of people here.'

But what if it's not enough? Zoe thought.

'Zoe!' Zoe heard Kerry call her name. 'Can you give me a hand with Stanley?'

'Coming!' Zoe called.

Her mum gave her a tissue. 'Here, dry your eyes. Everything will be all right. You'll see.'

Zoe really hoped Mum was right.

Chapter Twelve

'Come on in, everyone,' said Rory, holding the barn door open. It was the end of the day. All the visitors had finally left. Zoe and the others were exhausted. Kerry was sitting at her desk where she had been counting the money raised.

'I never want to brush another dog as long as I live!' declared Emily. Patch pressed against her legs. Emily rubbed her head. 'Well, apart from you, Patch.'

'And I am *so* glad my sponsored silence is over!' said Asha, throwing herself down on the sofa. 'It was horrible being quiet for so long!'

'You did raise £105 though!' said Rory.

'Maybe you should do it again next weekend!' teased Jack.

'No way!' said Asha.

Zoe sat down. The sofa felt wonderfully comfy after a day on her feet.

'I had lots of people come to watch my display,' said Jack. 'And they all put money into the bucket.'

'The grooming parlour was busy,' said Emily. 'And you said you had lots of people for riding lessons, Zoe.'

Zoe nodded and looked at Kerry who was being unusually quiet. 'But did we raise enough?'

Kerry rubbed her forehead and hesitated. Zoe's heart skipped a beat. Kerry heaved a deep sigh. 'I'm sorry, everyone. You've all worked so hard. I wish I had better news, but the truth is that although we've raised a lot we haven't raised enough.'

For a moment, there was total silence.

'No!' said Asha. 'After all that?'

'How much short are we?' asked Rory, his face crinkling in concern.

'About five hundred pounds,' said Kerry.

'Can't we ask Mr Jarvis to give us more time?' asked Zoe, her heart racing. 'Maybe we could do another fundraiser next week and raise the extra money then!'

'I doubt a second one would bring in as much money, Zoe. People like to give to good causes, but not every weekend,' said Kerry heavily. 'And anyway, I know Derrick Jarvis. He won't give us more time. If he's said we have to have the money by tomorrow then we have to have it by then. He'll take every excuse he can to make life difficult for us.'

Asha burst into tears. Emily put her arm round her. Zoe could feel tears in her own eyes too. *No*, she kept thinking. *It can't be happening.*

'I'm really, really sorry, everyone,' said Kerry.

Rory put a hand on her shoulder. 'At least we all know we tried,' he said. 'We didn't give up without a fight.'

'What ... what will happen to Swift?' Zoe forced the words out.

'I'll start ringing round and ask if anyone can take him in,' said Kerry.

Zoe couldn't bear it. Leaping to her feet she made for the door, forgetting her crutches in her unhappiness.

'Zoe!' Kerry exclaimed, jumping up, but Zoe was already out of the door, limping as fast as she could towards Swift's stable. She had to get to him. Tears welled in her eyes. She couldn't lose Swift. She couldn't!

'Zoe!' It was a different voice this time – her mum's voice coming from the direction of the car park.

Zoe kept going. She heard footsteps catching up with her and a hand caught her arm.

'Zoe, you haven't got your crutches!' her mum said. Seeing the tears streaking down Zoe's cheeks, she instantly looked concerned. 'What is it? What's happened?'

Zoe flung herself into her mum's arms. 'Mum, it's Swift!' she sobbed. 'We didn't raise enough money. He's going to go to a new home after all.'

'Oh, Zoe.' Her mum stroked her back and kissed her hair. 'Oh, sweetheart. That's awful.'

'I can't bear it, Mum!' The words burst out of Zoe. 'I'll never get to see him again if he goes somewhere else.' Her voice was drowned out by her sobs.

Her mum held her tight, stroking her hair. 'You're right. This isn't fair.' She took a breath. 'OK, look, you go and see Swift. I need to talk to Kerry and make a phone call.'

'Why?' Zoe felt a flicker of alarm. 'Not because I wasn't using my crutches?'

'No.' Mum laughed. 'It's lovely to see that your leg is so much better and I'm not certainly not cross with Kerry. You go on to the stables. I'll come and find you in a minute.'

Zoe hesitated, but right then all she wanted was to get to Swift. She carried on while her mum went down to the barn where everyone was clustered in the doorway.

As usual, Swift whinnied when he saw Zoe. She let herself into the stable and putting her arms round his neck, she gave way to the tears again. 'Oh, Swift,' she whispered. Swift snuffled curiously at her hair.

The fact he didn't know anything about what was going on cut through Zoe. He would get into the trailer, set off, and then they would never see each other again. She stroked him over and over again, wanting to make the most of every moment with him. She was going to miss him so much. How could she bear to watch him go? To come to the farm and not see him looking over his stable door? She felt like her heart was breaking.

Suddenly she heard the sound of voices. Swift pricked his ears. Zoe limped to the door and saw Asha, Jack, Emily, Kerry and Rory all walking towards the stable with her mum. She frowned. What were they all doing?

A horrible thought struck her. Maybe Kerry had found a home for Swift already and she was coming to tell her! But, no. Everyone was smiling. Surely they wouldn't be smiling if they were coming to tell her that?

'Can I tell her! Can I?' cried Asha, bouncing up

and down.

Kerry looked at Zoe's mum who nodded. 'Yes, you can tell her.'

Zoe came out of the stable as Asha raced over. 'Zoe! We can keep Swift!'

'What?' The world seemed to stop for a second for Zoe. 'Really? Why? How? What about the stable roof?'

'We can afford the new roof now!' exclaimed Asha.

'Well, we can if you want. It's up to you really,' Mum said cryptically.

'What do you mean?' Zoe asked.

'We got some compensation money from the accident,' Mum explained. 'Dad and I were going to give it to you, but we've just talked about it, and if you want we can donate some of it to City Farm to pay for the roof.'

Zoe stared at her mum. She was so shocked she couldn't speak. All she could do was nod as the tears spilled down her cheeks. This time they were happy tears.

Kerry, Jack, Emily and Rory beamed.

'Oh, Swift!' Zoe cried, flinging her arms round him. 'You can stay!' Swift snorted in surprise. Zoe kissed his face and laughed.

'Now, you're sure?' Mum teased. 'You wouldn't rather have a bike, or a new TV?'

'No way!' Zoe grinned. 'Being able to see Swift is the only thing I want. Except...' She stared at her mum. 'I want to be able to ride him too.'

Mum nodded slowly. 'I thought you might.' She took a deep breath. 'OK,' she agreed. 'When your plaster cast comes off, and your leg's *completely better* ... you can start riding Swift again.'

Zoe flung her arms round her mum. 'Thank you! Thank you so, so much!' she gasped. 'I'll be really careful. I promise.'

Her mum's eyes were bright with tears too. 'Just be happy – and keep dreaming. Dreams really can come true, you know.'

Zoe looked at Swift and smiled.

Epilogue

Swift trotted smoothly round the dressage arena, his chestnut neck arched, his strides even. Zoe sat deep in the saddle, her hands light on his reins and her chin up. Her new cream jodhpurs were spotless, her black riding jacket fitting her perfectly as she rode him through the dressage test she had learned over and over again every night in her bedroom. She was back upstairs now, and there were new posters on the walls – pictures of dressage riders and their horses.

Passing the judging box, Zoe moved her outside leg back and Swift surged into a canter. Zoe felt a thrill of delight. She loved cantering on him. To be able to go fast again felt amazing. It might not be her legs doing the running but it didn't matter. She cantered a perfect figure of eight and caught sight of her mum, watching from the side of the arena. *It's really happening*, Zoe thought excitedly, as she brought Swift smoothly back to a trot at the correct marker. *Our first dressage test and it's going so well!*

It was incredible to think that it was only a few months since she had started riding Swift. Kerry was delighted with the progress she was making. The physiotherapist Zoe was seeing for her limp had said that horse riding would be a great way to build up the muscles in her leg, and so it had been agreed that Zoe would ride Swift every day after school.

All the determination and dedication she'd once put into her running she was now putting into her riding and Swift was responding brilliantly. He loved doing dressage – just like she did.

They turned up the centre line to finish the test. Swift halted and stood obediently while Zoe dropped her hand to her side, bowing her head as she saluted the judge. Her breath rushed out of her. The test was over. She heard the clapping from the stands and let Swift walk out of the arena on a loose rein, his ears pricked.

As soon as she got outside, she jumped off and threw her arms round him, breathing in his sweet smell. 'You were brilliant, boy!'

Swift snorted happily, sharing her delight.

Her mum came hurrying over. 'Oh, Zoe! That was really great. He looked beautiful. I'm so proud of you!'

Zoe glowed. It was lovely having her mum at the competition supporting her, just like she had used to support her in her races. With her mum were two of her old athletics friends who had come along too to watch, just like Zoe had gone to cheer them on in their last race.

'I loved it!' she exclaimed. She kissed Swift's neck. 'And this is just the beginning, Swift – this is where it all starts!' Her eyes shone. She had so many dreams again now – so many things she wanted to achieve together with Swift.

Swift nuzzled her and she buried her face in his mane.

Whatever problems came along, as long as she had Swift, everything would be all right.

'It's you and me, Swift,' she whispered. 'For ever.'

CHARACTER PROFILE

ANIMAL: Horse

ANIMAL NAME: Swift

LIKES:

Galloping fast, being ridden by Zoe, being groomed.

DISLIKES:

Being bored.

FAVOURITE PLACE:

In the field with his friends, Stanley and Dusty.

FAVOURITE FOOD:

Apples and peppermints.

Turn over for a sneak peek of the next
City Farm adventure…

Darren and Basher

Art was Darren's favourite lesson. At least it was, until the day a man with a black beard came into the art room, carrying a large bowl of fruit. Darren had never seen him before.

'Where's Miss Hastings?' Darren asked.

Miss Hastings was the teacher who usually took the art class. She really liked Darren's artwork, and always had something good to say about it.

'You've got a great imagination, Darren,' she frequently told him, and sometimes she added: 'The way you use colours is fantastic.'

Art was the only thing he was any good at, since he'd first started at the secondary school, two years ago.

The black-bearded man plonked the bowl down in front of the class. It contained a bunch of grapes and a large melon.

'Making a fruit salad, sir?' asked Darren's mate Gary, who was sitting next to him.

The man frowned at Gary. 'Less of the cheek,' he said. Then he looked at Darren. 'Miss Hastings is off sick. Nothing serious, but she'll be away for the last two weeks of term. I'm Mr Dodge. I'll be taking over from today.'

'OK,' Darren said. Something told him he wasn't going to enjoy this new teacher's lessons. They wouldn't be fun, like Miss Hastings' lessons were.

He got out his rainbow-coloured felt-tips and laid them on the table in front of him. He always brought his own pens to the art class. With them, he could create the graffiti-style, super-bright effects he liked. He'd rather have used his spray cans, but they weren't allowed at school.

'You won't be needing those,' Mr Dodge said, eyeing the pens.

'But I always—' Darren began.

'Today you're going to be drawing a still life in pencil. The result must be realistic. It must reflect exactly what you see.'

Darren hated using pencils to draw. They were so dull and grey. And they were always breaking too.

'Still-life drawing is the foundation of all great art,' Mr Dodge said, as he walked around the class giving out paper and pencils. 'Da Vinci, Raphael, Picasso — they all began with the simple still life. I'll demonstrate for you.'

He set up an easel with a sheet of paper on it at the front of the class. Then he peered at the fruit bowl, and began sketching.

Darren sighed. This was so boring. He looked at Gary and yawned.

Gary sniggered. 'Let's go and smash that melon in,' he hissed. 'That'll make it more exciting.'

'Quiet!' Mr Dodge called. 'Still-life drawing requires concentration.'

Darren picked up the pencil he'd been given. He tried to copy exactly the way the melon looked, sitting on top of the fruit bowl, but he didn't like the way it came out. It looked lifeless, like something out of an art textbook.

He pushed harder with the pencil, trying to make a darker line, and the point snapped off.

'Sir, my pencil broke,' he said.

'Sharpen it, then,' Mr Dodge answered, still sketching.

Darren didn't have a pencil sharpener. He looked

around the class, but everyone was busy drawing. He didn't want to interrupt Mr Dodge again, so he got one of his felt-tips out. A bright purple one.

He used it to sketch the bunch of grapes. The cluster of shapes reminded him of a group of kids all huddled together in the playground, so he drew faces on them.

'Nice one, Daz!' Gary whispered, peering over his shoulder.

Darren turned his attention to the melon. He drew a big circle with a yellow felt-tip. Then he had an idea. He got a black pen, and added a beard and a pair of bushy eyebrows to the melon shape he'd just drawn.

It looked very like Mr Dodge now. Darren gave him arms, and a long paintbrush in one hand, as if the teacher had just painted the grape-kids' cheeky little faces.

Gary peered over Darren's shoulder and snorted with laughter.

Mr Dodge left the front of the class and came down to Darren's table. All the kids in the art class were looking at him, their eyes wide.

'Very amusing,' Mr Dodge said in his deep voice. 'But not what I asked you to do, is it?'

'It's loads better than your dumb drawing, sir. Daz

is a genius,' Gary piped up.

'Right, you, get out!' the teacher shouted. 'I won't have disrespect in my classroom. Go to the headmaster's office!'

Gary got up and shuffled out of the art room, turning to wink at Darren as he opened the door.

'Now, young man,' Mr Dodge continued, staring at Darren from under his bushy eyebrows. 'Either you do as you're told, or you'll be sent out too. An art class is no place for this kind of stupid scribbling.'

Darren felt anger bubble up inside of him. This was the one lesson he did well in. Now it was going to be just like all the rest. 'What do you know about art anyway?' he shouted, jumping up from his chair.

'Quite a lot, actually,' the teacher began. 'My paintings are very well known …'

But Darren wasn't listening. He didn't wait to be sent to the headmaster for being cheeky. He just ran out of the classroom, and hid behind the bike shed until it was time to go home.

Darren went to bed early, but he couldn't sleep. It was one of those nights in the middle of summer when it doesn't get properly dark until very late. He lay in bed, turning from side to side.

Mr Dodge's booming voice echoed in his ears. '*Stupid scribbling!*' Darren heard him say, over and over again.

But his graffiti-style felt-tip drawing was just as lifelike, just as realistic in its own way as the teacher's pencil sketch! It was so frustrating to be told off like that, for doing something that he knew he was good at.

At eleven o'clock, Darren heard his dad coming to bed. His mum was at work. She'd left just after tea to go to her night shift at the hospital. Soon his dad's snores could be heard through the bedroom wall. They were so loud they seemed to be shaking the whole flat.

Darren slid out of bed and put on his trackie bottoms and his trainers. Then he pulled his favourite hoodie over his head and picked up the shoulder bag with his spray cans in. There was only one way he was going to get Mr Dodge's voice out of his head.

He tiptoed out of his bedroom and went to the kitchen. The window in there looked out onto the walkway that ran outside all the flats on his floor. It was easy to open it and climb out.

He made his way through the silent, dark streets until he came to the entrance to his school. A light was on in one of the school's windows. Someone must have forgotten to switch it off, even though there were notices in every classroom reminding you to turn the light out when you left.

Darren made his way to the bike shed. Behind it was a long concrete wall. He'd seen it earlier, when he was hiding there. Darren's heart beat fast, like it always did when he was about to create a piece of art. He got out a green spray can and shook it.

Then he reached up as high as he could and began to outline some jagged shapes on the wall – palm tree leaves. In what seemed like only a few moments the concrete was transformed into a lush, green jungle.

Next, Darren grabbed a red spray can and began sketching in a troop of monkeys, swinging through the trees. He added a bigger monkey – himself, with his hoodie pulled forward to hide his face – chasing them with a spray can.

At the top he added *ART RULES* in big, bubble-style writing, and at the bottom he put his own special tag: *DAZ*. He always wrote this tag in hard-to-read, spiky letters, so that only someone who really understood graffiti would be able to read them.

He was just finishing the *Z* when he heard footsteps approaching. Someone must have spotted him!

Darren ran for the school gates, stuffing the spray cans back into the bag as he went. He was too late.

'Darren Taylor? Stop! What're you doing here at this time of night?'

It was the headmaster. He must've been working late. He always had to put in extra hours when he was working out the timetable for the next school year.

'You know that vandalizing school property is a very serious offence?' the headmaster said, coming up to Darren.

Darren shivered. If only he'd left the bike shed as soon as he'd finished drawing, and not added his tag. What was going to happen to him now?

Read

Darren and Basher

to find out what happens next!

Our *City Farm* and the *Harvest Hope* project
are fictional, but there are real city farms
all around the country and they often
need volunteers. Why not go and visit the
one nearest to you?